LITTLE HERCULES

LITTLE HERCULES

FRANCIS WALLACE

COACHWHIP PUBLICATIONS
Greenville, Ohio

Little Hercules, by Francis Wallace
© 2018 Coachwhip Publications

Published 1939
No claims made on public domain material.

CoachwhipBooks.com

ISBN 1-61646-435-6
ISBN-13 978-1-61646-435-6

CHAPTER I

Sitting at a ringside table in Hollywood's most pretentious night club, Terry Moore decided that America was just one big Saturday night town after all.

Most of the big names and big faces in pictures seemed to be on the small dance floor; yet they were enjoying themselves in much the same manner as the boys and girls of Sauk Center, Bellaire, Roaring Gulch, and Park Avenue—allowing always for variations in time, apparel, and cover charge—particularly the latter.

Here among themselves, they were human beings. Some closed their eyes while dancing, others talked. Occasionally they looked at Terry Moore as if trying to place him; when in doubt, they smiled; and he smiled, as if they were old friends.

Some of them were very old friends. He had been looking at them for a long time on the silver screen. Terry was still a fan, after ten weeks as a picture writer; but even the biggest picture people are picture fans, in tribute, perhaps, to the miracle they have never been able to comprehend, even though it has happened to them.

Dan Colby, sitting across the table, said:

"What I still can't understand is why any young fellow should want to walk out on all these dolls—to say nothing of the money!"

Terry answered: "And what I still can't understand is why a New York detective suddenly comes to Hollywood on vacation when he always went fishing before."

Dan Colby smiled, refilled Terry Moore's glass with champagne, watched the bubbles rise from the bottom of the stem to the surface. "It almost tempts me."

"Why don't you break over—since you're on vacation?"

Dan was a big, Dick Tracy type of man of about thirty-five; he had a heavy chin, a tackle's build, a panther's tread, and a strong pair of hands which he knew how to use. His strong, wide face broke into many wrinkles when he smiled or scowled, almost the same wrinkles, except for the small, determining ones about the eyes and mouth. He was a pleasant companion with orderly people; but his sense of humor sometimes took a sharp tangent when he was dealing with the people he called his boys and girls. He had a habit of inserting unpleasant topics into otherwise friendly discussions with them; of crunching their flabby hands, digging his strong fingers into their soft arms, of thrusting knuckles suddenly in their backs when they were off guard.

There was method in all this, as Terry Moore well knew. This was Dan's way of keeping them on their toes, of making them squirm, of never quite allowing them to forget that he was the law and they were outside the law. It was Dan's way of keeping fear in their hearts—fear of him—for Dan was the type of cop who liked to let them feel his weight. He could not ever let them think he was getting soft.

Perhaps this was in his mind, as he said, in a half-detached voice, while still watching the wine: "In your business, kid, the bubbly is fun. In mine, it's murder. So you have the fun. I'll pour you on the train in the morning."

"Nobody ever had to do that for me yet."

"I'm not telling you to start." Now Dan's face might have been caricatured with a series of slanting lines. "But somebody ought to enjoy Johnny's wine. When he cracks a bottle, he's giving his heart's blood. There are only two things John really cares about in this world— women and money; well, I should say three things, because John thinks quite a lot of himself, too."

"I never thought he'd let us in here."

Dan Colby laughed. "John and I have been pals for years. One of the toughest jobs I ever did was to chop up the old Golden Pheasant for him in New York. But I guess I did him a favor at that. He came out here and opened this little shack—quite a little shack." Dan's eyes centered on Terry. "I still don't get why you don't like this town."

"To anybody who likes New York, Dan, this is a foreign country. You'll get what I mean if you stay longer than three weeks. In the second place—it's not my racket. I had to find out about that—and I did."

"So now you're going back and draw pictures for the funny papers the rest of your life."

Terry was serious. "Nobody gave me much attention out here. I resented it for awhile—but now I appreciate it. They gave me time to think. And I've made up my mind about the two most important problems a young man has to decide. In fact, I've just about got my life all charted."

Dan smiled. "At the age of twenty-six. Terry, you're marvelous. What are these problems?"

"Career—and women."

"So there's a doll back home—eh?"

"Right."

"Well, I wish you luck, son." Dan looked over the crowd. "All I can say is, she must be some gal—to pull you back from all these biddies."

Terry was scornful. "Two things burn me up about this town more than anything else—what the men do to women—and women do to themselves. Just take a look around—and see all the young girls with old men."

"I've been covering Broadway for fifteen years, Terry."

"New York is puritanical, compared to this town."

"So they tell me." Dan looked about the sumptuous elegance of the Cinema Circle; at the subdued opulence of the supper room, done in Moorish blue; at the crystal brilliance of the bar, visible through the doorway. Everywhere were famous faces and famous names. Here was seclusion with class; a retreat where picture people could play in the same free atmosphere in which they worked. Here they could be people—and not servants of the people.

Dan marveled. "Yes, sir, you've got to give John a lot of credit. It's a long way from four-round bouts at the old Garden where I first saw him twenty years ago, to top man in the Hollywood gambling racket—with only one bad mistake." There was an odd note of sadistic affection in the detective's voice. "It would be too bad, in a way, if it caught up with him. In some ways the bum is marvelous. Just take a look at him now, coming from the bar—the guy with the shoulders— like a brewery horse in dinner clothes."

Terry knew Johnny Duke by reputation. He had fought as a middleweight. The years had made him into a heavyweight; but there was nothing about him that looked soft. His solid head was set close down upon unusually wide shoulders; his waist was slim and he had no tummy. Terry could believe the story that Johnny Duke still went to a gym every day to train.

A slow smile crept over Dan's face. "Yes, sir," he repeated, "in some ways the louse is marvelous. He hates my guts but he wants me to see how prosperous he is. He pretends he hasn't seen me yet but he knows every move I'm making." Johnny Duke's approach was slow. He stopped at many tables to chat, to pat arms, particularly feminine arms. Dan continued: "Funny guy, John. A little dancy on certain subjects. Right now he's trying to make out this is his house and all these nice people are his guests. Watch—now he's about ready to give me the gander."

To the people in the room, and some of them were watching very closely, the meeting between Johnny Duke and Dan Colby must have seemed a reunion of very old and very dear friends. They shook hands and hung on. They grasped each other by the arms and dug in—and for one fleeting moment, when their eyes told the truth, Terry thought they might come to grips, like wrestlers, and go to the floor.

But they sat down and talked like buddies.

"Nice place, John—got to hand it to you, son."

"Nothing like this in New York, eh, Dan?"

"You're right, John—not even the old Golden Pheasant."

Johnny smiled. "We don't have hatchet men out here, Dan. How come you honor us with your presence?"

"Oh, Broadway's dead since you left. All the big people are here, John. So I just thought I'd take my vacation time and get up on my stuff."

Terry suspected that there was an odd sort of affection between these two, based on a lusty hate that was chiefly a matter of direction. Dan, certainly, would have made a dangerous criminal; Johnny a cutely crooked cop.

They fenced like experts.

As always, when a new character interested him, Terry began to sketch Johnny Duke on the tablecloth. Johnny knew it, pretended that he didn't, but turned so that the artist would get his profile instead of the full face. There might have been many reasons for that. People in his position sometimes didn't like to be mugged; but Terry felt that, in this case, it might be because the front of his head was bald; he suspected that Johnny was sensitive about this because he had made the pathetic gesture of attempting to space the few strands of brown hair available there. From the profile the baldness was not apparent. Everything about Johnny indicated that he wanted to look young, and he did a good job. He must be almost forty; yet he might easily pass, even with the bald front, for thirty-five or under.

The swish of a skirt brushed Terry's knee. He looked up and square into the eyes of a red-headed girl who was dancing the rhumba. She gave him not more than a cold glance but his eyes followed her. She was a dramatic person, with one of the prettiest faces Terry had seen in Hollywood, and, certainly, a fine figure. But it was her hair and coloring that made her gorgeous.

She could dance. Each sensuous movement suggested some new part of her under the gold serpent cloth that flowed down from her deep breasts. Dan was watching, too. From the way Johnny Duke looked at her, Terry knew what kind of a man Johnny was with women; when she returned Johnny's gaze, Terry felt that he also had a slant on the girl.

"Like her?" Johnny asked Dan.

"A ditsy. Who's the boy friend?"

"Who do you think?"

"Still pickin' 'em, eh, John? I mean, who's the snake?"

Snake, Terry thought, was correct. The girl's dance partner was oily and handsome, too handsome; and much too old for this girl, who was about twenty-two.

"One of the locals—a Mex."

When the dance ended, the man and girl came to Johnny's table.

Dan spoke to the man. "Ever been to New York?"

"It is a pleasure I have missed." Ramon Toros had a slight accent.

Johnny chuckled. "Once your famous memory missed too, Dan. You've probably seen Ramon in pictures—he's been doing all right lately—and more than all right in my back room. Ruth, here, is his lucky charm—eh, sweetheart?" Johnny leaned over and rubbed his fingers at the base of her neck, among the warm fluff of her hair.

"You in pictures, Miss Allison?" Dan asked.

"She will be," Johnny said. "I'll see to that." He rubbed a thoughtful little circle in the flesh of her suntanned neck.

The same old story, Terry thought.

Then he wondered if the girl were a mind-reader. She was looking directly at him, as if she knew his thought and resented it. She had curious eyes—almost violet, with golden flecks. Terry had never seen the combination before. He thought he would like to paint them.

The girl said: "Johnny, have you seen this?" She indicated the sketch. Johnny pressed close to the girl, his arm snugly about her. Terry had double-crossed him by drawing the full face, with the strands across the bald spot. But Johnny enthused: "Well—what's this? Say, Dan, this kid can draw."

"I guess you didn't catch the name—Terry Moore."

"Why sure," Johnny said. "I should have known." But the name obviously didn't mean anything—nor to the others at the table.

Dan helped them. "He draws 'Little Hercules'—in the funny papers."

That registered. Johnny Duke looked at Terry with respect for the first time. "Owe you an apology, kid—I thought you were a cop." He grinned at Dan.

Dan was good-natured. "That's what I always liked about you, John—that touch of class—even back at the old Golden Pheasant. Ever hear of the Pheasant, Mr. Toros?"

Ramon Toros seemed to smile down at his cigarette. "On Fifty-fourth Street?"

Johnny explained. "He's heard me talk about it."

"Sorry we had to chop it up a little, John." Dan seemed genuinely sympathetic. "It was such a beautiful joint—paintings on the wall, velvet drapes—a man like you would have liked it, Mr. Toros."

"I'm sure I would have."

Ramon was amused. Johnny wasn't. His sharp eyes turned to the sketch. "Know what I'm going to do? I'm going to hang this picture on my wall."

Dan drawled. "It might be a bad omen, John. Remember Jesse James?"

Johnny turned to a waiter, spoke with sharp command. "Get Morgie."

Morgie was a big man with a hatchet face and a husky whisper of a voice. "Here, Morgie—cut this out—and be careful of my throat." Johnny laughed, a strangely lusterless laugh. "Whenever I have a job of cutting to do, I always call on Morgie. Look how neat his work is, even on a tablecloth."

"Very interesting," Dan Colby commented. "I've heard a lot about Morgie's work."

Morgie worked with a big pocketknife, did a neat job, held it up for a critical inspection. He was not entirely pleased. "It would look better with da hat," he said to Johnny Duke.

"You think so, Morgie?"

"Yeh—and more natural-like."

"Get the hat."

And so it was that Johnny Duke sat at midnight in his own club, wearing the favorite black hat that was almost his trade-mark, the hat which covered his baldness. People gathered around, twitted Johnny, who took it all good-naturedly and gave Little Hercules, if not Terry Moore, plenty of advertising—as he drew the hat on the tablecloth sketch. It became quite a little something, on this Saturday night at the Cinema Circle, and Terry Moore found himself taking bows in Hollywood from important people.

One of his fans, strangely enough, was Big Morgie, who was so neat with a knife. And another was Ruth Allison, who now looked at Terry Moore with different eyes.

"Here, Hercules," Johnny said, "suppose you autograph the picture—from Little Hercules to his pal, Johnny Duke—or something like that?"

Johnny stood back of Ruth Allison and rubbed the fingers of his two hands through her hair until Terry could think only of snakes and babies. Terry autographed the sketch from Little Hercules to his pal Johnny Duke, feeling that this definitely gave him an address on Phony Street; for if pal Johnny knew what pal Terry really felt about him, he might have Morgie do a neat job without cautioning him to be careful about the throat.

Morgie was ingratiating enough at the moment. There was almost pleading in his shadow voice: "Hey, Hercules, how about drawin' me in there every day to help out da little guy? I'm just the kind of guy he needs in the pinches."

"Okay, Morgie—I'll drop around some day and get the story of your life."

Dan Colby chuckled. "When you do, let me have a copy. Interesting reading, don't you think, Mr. Toros?"

Ramon Toros inspected his polished nails. "I dare say, Mr. Colby, I dare say."

Johnny, watching them, said: "I'll tell you a story on Morgie. One of the boys got caught with the double cross—as they always get caught—and the man he cheated cut it out of his heart—to remember him by."

Johnny's voice was sharp.

There was electric stillness at the table. Ramon was lighting a cigarette.

Now a smile broke upon Johnny's face, as if he were coming to the really good part of the story. "Well, a committee was delegated to tell the widow. One of the boys was trying to break it gently, but Morgie here got impatient—remember, Morgie? Tell 'em what you said."

Morgie's laugh was like a bad cough. "Oh, I just said, 'What's da use beatin' round da bush, Mabel—you and the two kids got a tough break—Bootsie just went bye-bye'."

Johnny's laugh was like a sound in an empty house.

Dan Colby asked: "Bootsie didn't happen to be the night watchman at the Golden Pheasant, did he, Morgie"

Morgie turned, in obvious alarm, to Johnny Duke. The latter said: "Never mind Dan—he's just here on vacation."

Dan's voice was pleasant. "You never know when you might grab a brass ring—eh, Mr. Toros—"

Ramon said, "Sometimes when one least suspects—"

Johnny cut in quickly. "Sometimes it slips up on you, Ramon. You can't be too careful." His hands were running quickly now, probably unconsciously, through the girl's hair.

"Johnny—" she objected—"you'll ruin my hair-do."

His low voice was almost a gurgle. "Now wouldn't that be too bad if I ruined—your hair-do?"

Johnny laughed and Morgie laughed.

Terry Moore left the table.

The others watched him go.

Terry walked to the bar, took an empty stool, looked at the mirror. He could see the table he had left. The girl was still watching him. He could not get the expression on her face but decided it would probably be hard or merely expertly vacant.

He couldn't stand any more of Johnny Duke and his hands in her hair; of women who looked like angels and acted like tramps. She hadn't given him a tumble until she found out he drew Little Hercules, that he was somebody in the peerage of Hollywood.

The bartender was asking what he wanted. Terry said Scotch. He looked into the mirror.

The bartender was asking how he wanted it.

Ramon Toros and Ruth Allison were leaving the table.

"Give it to him barefoot," a girl next to Terry was saying.

"Okay?" the bartender asked.

"Okay." Terry turned to the girl. This one was all touch-and-go, with no hidden depths to plumb. It was right out there on the counter, take it or leave it. She was slim and cup-breasted; her eyes and face were small—but nothing about her was too small. She was all gal and she knew it and she used it. She was a deep brunette and her eyes were looking into his. Her eyes were dark with storm.

She was easy to talk to—so easy that Dan Colby found them, somewhat later, with heads close together, obviously intent upon a matter of moment. The detective wedged between them, said gruffly: "Come on, break it up, bums."

The girl's ruffled reaction was softened by Terry's grin. She asked, pleasantly enough: "Who is this elephant's heel?"

"The best detective in New York," Terry answered. "Dan, this is Judy."

Judy was unimpressed. "What's he doing out here?"

"On vacation—ses he."

"Then why don't he vacate?"

Dan chuckled. "Keep punchin', Judy."

"Go away, flatfoot. We're workin' on something."

"What's the plot?"

Terry explained. "We're going to insult her boy friend. He's a heel. He went off with another woman and left this poor kid alone at the bar. There he is over there."

"Why, the dirty louse! Let's go get him."

"Okay." Terry was off the stool. Dan had his arm.

Judy protested. "Hey—you're going the wrong way."

"Keep punchin', Judy," Dan winked. To Terry he said: "For a guy who claims to have his life all charted, you're doing all right."

CHAPTER II

The liquor was obviously in Terry Moore but it released a charm and warmth that made him an attractive human being. His eyes were friendly but inconclusive; brown eyes that were neither shy nor bold, but like those of a reckless boy willing to play any game that had fun in it. His hair, of the same indeterminate brown as his eyes, was plentiful and inclined to be unruly. He did not look like a young man who was walking into the shadow of a guillotine.

They left the bar and foyer—a stratosphere of soft blue lights, of rich drapes, bubbling voices, and bright flushed, handsome, famous faces. The light gayety fled before something vital, something with the quality of physical fight, of a meeting of enemies, of serious sex.

It was the feel of big money, of gambling, of lawbreaking—the feel of the illicit, of the old speakeasy days in New York.

Dan Colby's eyes were keenly alert, missing nothing. A man in a dinner coat stood at the entrance to an unobtrusive corridor. His cold eyes covered them, as they passed through. Terry knew that he was armed, as he knew that Dan was armed, knew that each of these men had mentally searched the other. There were a few pictures on the wall, copies of the masters, further evidence of Johnny's touch of class. Two more men in dinner coats, on guard at the other end of the corridor, unmasked themselves with vulgar underworld oaths, although they seemed to be talking of nothing in particular. The long corridor, reminding Terry of a bridge of sighs, a dressed up bridge, opened into an anteroom with *credit* and *cash* wicket windows.

The gambling room itself was probably sixty feet by thirty, with a suggestion of division in the center. The rich exuberance of the rest of the house was also there. There were tables for roulette, craps, black-jack and a bird cage or two. It was like a big movie set of such a scene before rehearsal, at one of those lolling moments when the players and mechanics were at ease. Ease was definitely the word for this place. The house men were pleasant, even quietly jocular. The players were poised, without a suggestion of the tension which is assumed to accompany big gambling. Two old ladies, sprawled on chairs in a corner, were unconscious comic relief. They had probably come from curiosity and were waiting for somebody to take them home. Their faces were tired and, probably, their feet, for these were heavy ladies.

Terry came upon Ruth Allison and Ramon Toros at a roulette wheel. The girl was keeping notes on a pad; and the man seemed to be playing a system based on the notes she kept. A crowd was watching. Terry remembered what Johnny had said about Ramon being on a winning streak. Terry began to play with Ramon, who nodded friend-ly recognition. He was soon wiped out. The girl's smile annoyed him. He bought more chips, returned to the table with every indication of a man who intended to get even.

The girl frowned. Terry hesitated, did not bet. Ramon lost. The girl smiled faintly. This time Terry bet—and won. Ramon started to lose steadily, but now Terry was not playing Ramon. He was playing a woman's smile.

People were watching him now, instead of Ramon. Each time the ball careened like a little world through orderly space, his heart pounded, but he sat on his emotions. He was feeling a queer sort of nervousness. He was trying not to betray the breathless excitement he felt each time his fingers stacked the chips.

Johnny Duke's voice broke from behind. "A high-roller, eh, Her-cules?"

"Beginner's luck," Terry answered.

Johnny looked at Terry's stack, then at Ramon's. He ran his fin-gers through Ruth Allison's hair. "Looks," he said cheerfully to Ra-mon, "like she's turning the luck against you tonight."

Ramon shrugged good-naturedly. "Well, Hercules," Johnny con-tinued, "I like to see my pals get it—but don't make me pay too much for that picture." He laughed and his hands rumpled the girl's hair.

Her face seemed to catch the flame from her hair. She frowned; shook her head as if to free it from his touch. Johnny's fingers tightened. Terry thought the fingers were actually putting pressure on the girl's throat.

"Kind of touchy tonight, aren't you, sweetheart?" Johnny's laugh had the vacant-house quality again.

Across the strained silence at the table, Terry's voice cracked: "Then why don't you keep your hands off her?"

Play seemed to stop everywhere at the unaccustomed noise. When it was seen that Johnny Duke was involved, there was a slow movement toward the table from all over the room.

Terry felt actual danger for the first time in his life. His body and mind froze to attention. He saw and felt everything about him—even though he dared not take his eyes from those of Johnny Duke. Johnny's eyes, killer-gray, were leaping angrily in their fleshy caves. The skin over the bald, bony forehead was stirring restlessly. Terry knew that to show fear was the surest way to be bitten by a mad dog. So he fought Johnny Duke's eyes with unexpected strength. His right arm was tensed, ready to uppercut, even straining to go; his fist was an iron rock he was getting ready to throw. Terry was surprised, pleased, and then proud, to find that, while he wanted desperately to get out of this, he was not going to crawl out of it.

Perhaps this was what Johnny Duke saw. He did not swing; he did not curse; he gave Terry a stabbing look, growled: "Get out of here—and stay out."

"That's okay with me." Terry's voice was steady enough, but when he started to collect his checks, his nervous fingers dropped one to the floor. Nobody bothered to pick it up.

Ramon Toros was stroking his chips as though nothing much had happened, but the glance he gave Terry under lidded eyes was approving. Morgie was nearby, looking at Johnny Duke.

Terry began to feel quaking fear, to realize just what he had blurted himself into.

Then Dan Colby strode into the middle of the situation and took charge. "Get your money," he said to Terry. He turned to Johnny Duke. "What's the matter—can't you take it any more?"

Johnny snarled. "You're not in New York now, Dan."

Dan's teeth bared in a humorless smile. "Ever think of taking a trip back, John?"

"I'll let you know when I do."

"Maybe I'll let you know. Tell your gorilla here, who cuts so neat with a knife, that goes for him, too. And one thing more, this kid came here with me tonight and he's going home with me. I'm taking over his argument, whatever it was."

Ruth Allison watched them leave. Her lips were slightly apart but her face was without emotion. Terry felt that she looked upon him as a young goof.

They drove west on Sunset. Dan watched the traffic behind until he seemed satisfied that they were not being followed; then he grinned at Terry Moore.

Terry smiled self-consciously. "Just as well you came along when you did—but it took you long enough."

Dan chuckled. "Don't tell Dewey—but I was in a crap game. I was piling up a little velvet when I heard that big quiet and saw you looking down Johnny's throat. You were doing all right, Hercules."

"I was scared."

"Well, you kept your chin up; but you're not safe running around these bistros. You're a pushover for these wacky dolls."

"I wouldn't say that."

"In my business all I go on is what I see. I asked you to go out with me for a peaceful evening, thinking you were a quiet, peaceful guy. You get loose, meet up with a barfly and in ten minutes this little Judy has you trying to insult one of the biggest gees in the movie business."

Terry grinned. "It seemed the thing to do at the time."

"You shouldn't mix Scotch and champagne. You would have been sure pop to wind up with a Michael Finn or a bat on the head. Anyhow, I get you out of that and in no time at all you are trying to break the bank and sounding off to one of the real tough guys left in the rackets. What happened?"

"I got tired watching him paw that girl."

Dan shook his head. "You could see what she was, couldn't you?"

"I'm not so sure about that. Did you get a good look at her eyes?"

"Listen, kid. There has been many a good man ruined by the right look from the wrong doll's eyes."

"Women write history with their eyes, Dan."

"Right—but the kind of history written by dolls who hang around night clubs is all bad—from Salome on down to this redhead. Let them fight their own battles."

"Not very chivalrous, are you?"

"Not since I was fifteen and sat on a bimbo's lap on a burlesque stage. I have been looking at these tramps all my life—they're a dime a dozen and that's all they're worth."

"I still don't think she is a tramp."

"All right—give her all the best of it. Say she's sweet and pure as the baby's milk—but she's sitting on a hot spot if ever I saw one. If you move in for her, you are sure pop to get burned."

"I'll never see her again."

"Maybe that's just as well. Some women have funny effects on some guys—and this one looks like bad medicine for you. Maybe you've been drawing that guy in the funny papers so long you begin to act like him—but if you're smart you'll let Little Hercules take all the raps. They won't hurt him."

They rode along quietly for a while. Then Dan asked: "How did Ramon act during this argument with Johnny?"

"I had a feeling he was with me. He's a Mexican, isn't he?"

"Mexican, hell! He's Brooklyn white trash."

Terry laughed. "Take it easy. My girl lives in Brooklyn."

Dan did not answer. He seemed to be thinking. After awhile Terry asked: "What was all the talk about the Golden Pheasant?"

Dan's voice was clipped. "Just talk."

"Never did find out who killed that night watchman there, did you?"

"No."

"But you're working on a new lead, aren't you? Wasn't that why you went out to Johnny's place tonight? Is Ramon mixed up in it?"

"I said I was on vacation."

"You can't stop me from wondering."

The lobby of Terry's hotel was deserted. Dan said: "It's too early for me to get to bed. I'll go up and have a nightcap."

Terry grinned: "Since I seem to need a bodyguard, maybe it's just as well I'm leaving town tomorrow."

"Nothing like that. Johnny's smarter than he used to be. He is sitting pretty out here and he's not looking for trouble, particularly with newspaper men or any of my friends. But it won't do any harm to keep your left out in case you meet him again. He is a big-feeling guy and you cut him tonight where it really hurt. You called him in public and made him look bad in front of a doll; then you got away with a chunk of his dough—and he won't like that. If he ever should make a pass at you, bluff it out, like you did tonight, then get in touch with me. And you'd better forget anything you heard tonight. This kind of stuff is not your dish. Just do like I told you—go back and marry Miss Brooklyn and leave the business of rescuing the damsels in distress to Little Hercules."

At 11 o'clock in the morning Terry Moore followed the porter through the stadium-like station at Los Angeles, toward the shiny monarch of stainless steel which was to carry him back to New York. There was a certain ceremony about the departure of one of these high-speed trains. This one was called The Giant, probably after the fabulous fellow in the seven-league boots. The scene, Terry decided, was faintly operatic, with self-conscious principals and the chorus which had come to sing farewell. He would write that to Luella. She liked that sort of stuff.

Far down the track he saw a girl who reminded him of Ruth Allison. He chuckled at the reaction on Luella had she been called upon to read in this morning's New York papers that Terry Moore had caused a sensation at the swanky Cinema Circle by engaging in an argument with sinister Johnny Duke—an argument over a soiled dove of Hollywood, at that.

Luella would have found it all very difficult to understand—as Terry himself was having difficulty in this bright light of the morning after. Strange, the different way things looked in the bright light of Sunday morning and the bright lights of Saturday night—or the eerie blue lights of alcohol, more likely.

But now it was farewell to all that—to Hollywood and its synthetic glory, its slapped-on glamour, its mythical gold, its pirates in dinner clothes. Back to New York where he belonged, to Luella. Terry had a warm glow every time he thought of Luella; certainly, in the cool influence of her serenity, there would be an end to such foolishness as sounding off to racket tops and drinking barefoot Scotches at bars with pretty but rebellious little dolls.

He vengefully wiped his feet on the concrete soil of California for what he thought would be the last time, fully convinced that one phase of his life was over and another was about to begin.

Which proved to be true enough, after a fashion.

A telegram was waiting in his compartment.

ABOUT TIME YOU ARE COMING HOME DEAD-
LINE NEW SERIES FRIDAY HERCULES GASP-
ING FOR AIR FOUR MORE PAPERS CANCEL THIS
WEEK BETTER COME UP WITH AN IDEA OR YOU
ARE SUNK REGARDS

                                          CARMICHAEL

CHAPTER III

The trouble with Carmichael was that he had a Hollywood obsession. He swore that the movie people waited until he had built up a name, then gobbled the name and ruined it. They were never the same, Carmichael preached, after they had been to Hollywood. He didn't know what happened to them. All he knew was that it did. He started to quit on a man, he always said, as soon as he stepped on the train going west.

This was Carmichael, who wouldn't hesitate at a little thing called misrepresentation if it would save an artistic soul—or an Empire Feature. Carmichael had to be discounted—but there was no need for him to get so insulting about it. Hercules had lost a few papers, so what? All business was slipping.

Now that he was through with Hollywood, Terry would show Carmichael how to buck the trend. He would make Carmichael eat that telegram some day—actually eat it. And the time to start was now. His mind began to glow. He took a rectangular drawing board from his pullman case, set it across his long thighs, which made a convenient easel. It was good to be back on the old rock pile again, hammering out some fantastic melodrama with sufficient human interest and comedy to last three weeks.

He pounded at the rocks in his head, searching for the elusive idea which would springboard Little Hercules on another humorous labor for the benefit of his fellow-men. The idea was for Herky to stick his long little nose into some mess which was none of his business at all; to get kicked around for his trouble; then to come out of it right side up, head bloody but unbowed. It would all be a little droll and quite goofy; but it would be enjoyed by people who loved to see the villain foiled and the maiden saved—by those who had too much sense to get mixed up in such foolishness themselves. Anyhow, it was the prescription which had made Little Herky a hero to 40,000,000 readers of 276 papers—234 papers now!

An hour later Terry Moore stared at the passing Santa Anita race track. On the paper before him was only the figure of Herky himself, with his thin little body and long, amiable narrow face caricatured until it resembled an inverted pear. Herky was there—but he wouldn't spark. And now Terry began to fear that Carmichael might be right—to wonder if either he or Herky had really sparked during their stay in Hollywood.

Terry laid the drawing board aside. Best to wait until something popped out of his head, some little quick illumination which, if you put a match to it, would warm the mind and set the imagination to glow. Ideas that were labored over were usually just labored ideas; which was just about what was wrong with Hollywood.

He turned to his portable radio and tried for music. But it was still Sunday morning and all he could get was sermons. They were not his kind of sermons but he listened. After all, it was Sunday morning; but after awhile he gave up. The preachers all talked like producers—they gave out the same old stuff.

The train stopped at San Bernardino. He watched the people move around the platform, all the little dramas of good-by, of putting in time. He saw a girl with a figure like a streamlined Venus walking away from the newsstand. There was something familiar about her. He speculated upon how much the back of a person tells about the front—little details of grooming which tell the story of a mind and sometimes the story of a face.

The train climbed into desert country.

Herky wouldn't perk.

Terry started to design a desert shack for him and Luella, with a sleeping porch for her asthma and a studio for him. He could work just as well out here as in New York—he might even work better—there would be less diversion. And once in the same house with Luella, there would be no shirking work.

Luella didn't think much of Hercules. She was a librarian who did book reviewing on the side, used words like generic and talked like an editorial writer. She tolerated Hercules only as a step toward greater things. She was always urging Terry toward greater things. He had an idea Luella was kidding herself, trying to convince herself that she was going around with a significant artist instead of a mug who had graduated from sports cartoons to the funny papers.

Not that Luella was all culture. She was pretty and she could dance—she was all girl when she let herself go, which, however, wasn't often enough.

Right now, for instance, Terry was getting damned good and mad with himself and Little Hercules because the idea wouldn't come for the new series. His madness spread to everything about him—the train, the interminable desert scrub, the occasional railroad stops they called towns, Carmichael, Johnny Duke, Ramon Toros, Ruth Allison—

Luella would have given his mood some psychological interpretation, would have used it to prove that Hercules was merely the momentary expression of his creator's acute sense of justice. Terry would have insisted that he was just damned good and mad and would have put it on all the more; and Luella would have grown calmer than ever, and acted like a doctor humoring a screwball patient.

But Terry knew there was some method in his madness, as he suspected there was some in everybody's madness. Once, as a boy, burned by some small caging, he had walked around the block and indiscriminately damned every damned house on the damned street. It had seemed to bring some relief. Ever since that time this had been his method of breaking a mental log jam. When his mind quit on him he followed his instincts. This, he knew, was why a lot of people thought he was slightly screwy; but his instincts had never led him into any serious trouble. Even last night, deep down in the engine room of his subconscious, he had probably realized that Dan Colby was nearby before he had allowed himself the luxury of sounding off to Johnny Duke.

His mind drifted in a delicious doze. He hadn't slept so well last night. Events of the dynamic evening were recreated in his imagination. He had kept his chin up, as Dan had said, and Terry was a little proud of that now. But, after all, he *had* acted like Hercules; he *had* stuck his nose in business that was none of his own—and dangerous business. The fact that Dan, who was no alarmist, had thought it necessary to see him to his room, was proof of that.

Terry had gone out of his way to cross a murderer. He was quite sure of that, now. Dan Colby was not in Los Angeles on any vacation. Two years ago the night watchman of Johnny Duke's Golden Pheasant had been killed. Dan had been on that case. It had never been solved. A burglar was supposed to have committed the crime. But, shortly after, Johnny Duke, with his henchman Morgie, had left town and settled in California.

Dan had arrived in town yesterday. He had immediately gone to Johnny's new place. He had prodded all of them about the Golden Pheasant. Ramon was mixed up in it. When Dan had quizzed Ramon, Johnny had been stung into telling the story about Morgie. Dan had practically accused Morgie of murdering the night watchman, Boot-sie. Morgie had been alarmed and Johnny had tried to cover that up.

And Terry had stuck his nose in this mess because of a girl who was obviously Ramon's girl—or Johnny's girl. Why? Because his instinct had told him that the girl was not quite what she seemed to be. This may have been one time when his instinct had slipped up. Today the girl was much on his mind. He was continually seeing women who reminded him of her. Maybe Dan was right. Maybe it was just as well that Terry was to see no more of Ruth Allison.

Anyhow, it was good to be on this train, going away from all that, back to Luella, bless her, and to Little Hercules—damn him, why wouldn't he perk?

The radio switched to a news program—the usual routine culled from the day's events throughout the nation. Hitler said something, so did Roosevelt. The Democrats were going to nominate Farley, after all, as a compromise candidate. Business prospects were improving. A man had been found killed in a downtown office building in Holly-wood. A fire was raging in Kansas City—stuff like that.

Little people ran in Terry's dream, danced on his brain to music mad and sweet, brought up from the fresh green graves of recent things, fantastic lights and figures.

Then, in the manner of dreams, there flashed from the misty vac-uum a brilliant spark that came from the distance as a comet comes to earth, and with a comet's swish, searing his mind with a forceless flame that stirred him back to consciousness.

Terry was on his feet so quickly awake, but so partly asleep, that his mind caught the tail of that dream. He talked to himself, paced the small room, holding fast to the spark, warming it until it took form in his mind, ran riot over his imagination and finally began to make his fingers itch.

He sat in the chair with the drawing on his knees and went to work. He scrawled sudden notes on the margins, occasionally rubbed his hands, talked to himself as he worked.

"Nice girl—wrong people—Herky sticks his nose in, gets punched around but defeats Black Knight and rides away on the trusty charger—formula okay—first part in the Cinema Circle setting the stage; middle on the train—escape, flight, pursuit—then the windup in New York. . . . Seems to fit. . . . Backgrounds—gambling casino, streamlined train—"

Terry snapped his fingers with a swinging motion of his arm. "Streamlined. That's what the strip needs. That's what we'll give them. . . . Gambling is as hot now as bootlegging was. . . . Same background, same type of people—we've got something, Herky, old boy—"

He thumbed his nose ecstatically: "For you, Carmichael."

Then he gradually became less the drunken creator and more the rational workman. "Now we've got to figure out just what a nice girl was doing mixed up with rats." He sketched Ruth Allison's face on the board. "Well, she might have been doing a lot of things—that's easy enough. But whatever it is, she gets herself in the switches between two rats. It isn't just love the two bums fight over—something else—"

He sketched Ramon Toros, with his sheikish face, and then Johnny Duke, chuckling as he added the black hat. "There you are, Johnny boy. . . . Sure—they quarrel over dough—Johnny is nuts over two things—women and money. Okay, they fight over money—uh—oh—" He pondered, played the end of his nose like a zither, then: "Why not? If we're going to make it tough, let's make it tough—that guy who was found dead, in an office building today—that's Ramon or Johnny, makes no difference now—figure that our later—and that's why the girl is running away. She didn't do it, of course, but circumstantial evidence is too strong and she blows. Happens to take same train as Herky, which is where we came in."

He leaned back, lit a cigarette, nodded to himself. "Stick Herky in the middle of that—" With a few quick strokes he made Hercules stand up on the paper—the thin little man with the head like an inverted pear—"and chuck Dan in there to give him a little help now and then. Morgie's idea—funny where you get the ideas in this business."

He looked in the mirror, talked to himself. "What's wrong with that? Nothing, you dope. It's perfect. It's terrific. So what're we waiting for?"

He worked slowly, carefully at first, then as the creative flame flared, with speed and excitement. He mumbled as he worked, spoke the lines of the dialogue, acted out the parts. In his concentration he was oblivious of the drum of the train; he lived in the spirit world of the artist, forgot the practical world, forgot more of it, he was to discover later, than was wise.

When three drawings were finished, he sealed the strips in a special long envelope and spent some time in composing an insulting telegram to Carmichael. At the next stop he mailed the strips and sent the wire. Then, because nobody buys as many papers as a newspaperman, he drifted to the newsstand. There he came upon the streamlined Venus. She was wearing sun glasses and her hair was covered with a scarf; but this was Ruth Allison—unless there were two of her, for she was looking at him exactly as he had left her last night, with lips apart.

She had very sensitive lips.

CHAPTER IV

The curve in a girl's upper lip can be as attractive and distinctive as a dimple in her chin, and much more expressive. Now the curve in Ruth Allison's lip told Terry Moore she was as surprised as he, and much more agitated.

Terry took her arm. "I've got a radio in my room," he said.

"What—no etchings?" Her voice was cool and low and a trifle throaty—the right kind of a voice for her face and figure and hair. Terry was always disturbed when a voice didn't match a personality —like Morgie, for instance; although Morgie's thin groan of a voice might have some significance at that.

Like most people who have something vital to talk about, they had difficulty getting started. Terry fiddled with the radio. She sat on the long divan. She had removed the glasses and hair kerchief and Terry decided that, at least, he had made a fool of himself over a good-looking woman. Looking out the window she seemed to know that he was appraising her, and obligingly held the pose.

He started with her legs, of course, although he wasn't rude about it nor did his eyes linger. Slender legs were as much to be expected on a girl like this as on a thoroughbred filly. She was wearing meshed hose—expensive, he thought, although he really didn't know. Her hands and arms were nice. She didn't drip her nails in red ink every morning. They were the approximate shade of her lips, which did not bleed either but were like pink petals. Close up, this way, she was even more attractive than at night.

You must understand Terry's preoccupation with bone structure and shadings of color because he was an artist. He suspected, too, why she hadn't clicked in Hollywood. The camera is a fickle, untruthful instrument which exaggerates. Features which are naturally beautiful sometimes register a trifle too big—and those which lack some natural beauty in themselves often come blooming through the camera. This girl, prettier than most stars in Hollywood, was a symbol of the cinema which consistently rejected perfection for something with a flaw—and tried to cover the flaw with glamour.

Her eyes were full upon him now, her voice was frank and her manner disconcerting. "Finished, Mr. Artist?"

"You've posed before?"

"Some."

"Where?"

"New York—and Hollywood."

"We should get along very well. Your face is just about right, I would say. In fact, I've already used it in one of my strips."

"Really? With Little Hercules?"

"I hope you don't mind?"

"I should be flattered, shouldn't I?"

"I'm not so sure about that; but I couldn't resist the urge. You were just the type."

She studied him, seriously now, as if fully to get his meaning.

He blurted out: "I'm sorry about last night."

"I'm not."

If Terry wrote to Luella about such experiences as this, which he never did, he would tell her what he was now seeing—a woman coming slowly to bloom, as a rose at morning. Ruth Allison's eyes seemed to expand, to become more entrancingly disturbing; the curve of her lip made a shy smile. And now her voice was a glowing current on silver wires, with just that trace of husky static. "I think I know where Little Hercules came from."

"If you mean what I think you mean, I resent that."

"I meant it to be nice."

"But Herky is a nut, a screwball—"

"He is a modern knight."

"He is a dope who gets punched around—"

She smiled. "Mr. Moore—I just won't have you picking on my hero."

He chuckled. "Well, maybe you know him better than I do."

"Maybe I do."

"You talk like Luella."

Her tone changed and her eyes. "Oh—I see. And who is Luella?"

"A girl."

"Just a girl?"

"Well, yes and no."

"What does she look like?"

"Well, she's tall and blonde and sort of stately and beautiful. Yes, I suppose you'd have to say Luella was quite beautiful."

"Not quite the type you would meet at a gambling table." Her voice was metallic.

He was defensive. "She's no smack, if that's what you mean."

"Suppose she had read in the paper this morning that her boy friend got in a jam over a Hollywood redhead—"

He grinned. "I was thinking of that."

"She wouldn't like it, would she?"

"No, I don't suppose she would—but on the other hand, you never can tell about Luella. You see, she reasons from general principles."

She glanced at the rack above. "She won't like that feather in your hat."

"How did you know?"

"And she'll tell you not to wear those tweeds in town, as they do in Hollywood; and she suggests places for you to go—and sort of guides your reading—doesn't she?"

Terry was looking at her with an awed smile. "You're not a fortune teller, are you?"

She leaned forward and took his hand. Her fingers were warm but not so feverish as Judy's had been. But Judy had been drinking bare-foots—and so had Terry.

Now, as Ruth studied his hand, Terry looked closely at the gold strands of her hair, followed them to their roots, saw no sign of dye, felt a bit ashamed of his curiosity but justified himself by deciding that women brought such masculine inquisitiveness on themselves. He studied her neck, her ears, the back of her head. He was conscious of a subtle fragrance that came from the girl and not from any per-fume—

He heard: "A redheaded stranger has come into your life—"

He said: "A beautiful stranger with hair the shade of a copper rose—"

"You must avoid this redhead—"

"I don't see why—"

"She brings you trouble—"

"I could stand a little more such trouble—"

His fingers closed over hers. She straightened them out, said, "I see a stately, beautiful blonde—"

"Let's leave her out of this—"

"But does she want to be left out?"

He said: "You'd look great in technicolor."

"Mr. Moore, you wear a mask. You pretend to be bashful and earthy—but you batter at a girl's weakness like a sly Casanova."

"Wise to my system, are you?"

"You lure with flattery—but hide all the while behind the goddess Luella." She dropped his hand, smiled at him with friendly understanding, took a cigarette and lit it. Her voice was now well-trimmed with husk. "Mr. Moore, you are a phony. I seal my heart and my lips—against you."

She crossed her heart and her lips. He pretended great confidence, said: "It's a long way to New York." He opened a sport bag, came up with a long-stemmed pipe which he filled from an involved slicker-pouch with ritual movements.

She said, "I suppose you blend that tobacco yourself."

"How did you know?"

"I sort of thought you would."

They had reached a milestone of acquaintance, realized it, and were going through the process of shifting gears. Seeming finally and definitely to come out of a nervous contortion, she stretched comfortably on the divan and flexed like a doeskin cat. Terry flopped in the chair with the abandon of a rag animal. His right leg was over a chair arm at right angles to his left; he looked at her carefully over the large smokestack of his pipe.

"So you read Hercules?"

"Every day."

"Have you noticed him falling off?"

She hesitated. "No-o."

"But you haven't been excited about him lately."

"He's just satisfying—with a slow sort of charm."

"Well, he's been laying down on me. I've been working all day trying to get an idea."

"Am I keeping you from work?"

"No—I finally got the idea. It's the one I used you in."

"Could I see it?"

"I just sent the first strips off. You'll see them in the papers in about a week."

"I'll be watching."

She was nervous again. The fingers of her right hand were running little races along the seat. Terry's right forefinger slowly twanged across the point of his long nose. They were silent for awhile, and each knew they were closing in on the thing they had to talk about.

She said: "Why do you play your nose like a zither?"

"Same reason, I imagine, as you run races with your fingers. I'm thinking—or trying to."

"About last night?" When he did not reply, she staged another race with her fingers, this time deliberately and in slow motion. "See how the middle one always wins?"

"It's the longest."

She nodded, soberly. "There's a long finger in every gambling game. They call it the house edge. Over the long run no player can beat it." Her lids came up slowly from the racing fingers. He saw that her eyes could be sad.

"You seem to know a lot about gambling."

"I should, I suppose, since I've been in the racket myself." Her voice was bitter.

"I can hardly believe that."

"I couldn't either, at first—but that's another thing you learn in gambling—that you can't kid yourself out of a cold fact. I thought I had the house edge running with me. When I found that it was against me, I checked out. That's why it's so odd that I should meet you again—because you let me know what I was up against."

"Then it was the blind leading the blind."

"I saw it first in your eyes when I was dancing with Ramon; it was there when we met; I saw it again when Johnny was pawing me. At first I was terribly annoyed; but when I learned that you drew Little Hercules, I began to understand. I knew why you left the table—and when you came back to gamble, I saw you had been drinking and I was afraid you were going to lose heavily—and that, somehow, it would be because of me. Then Johnny came again and you said what you did."

"I should have kept still."

She nodded. "Yet you did it. You made me feel that if a stranger could think that way about me, perhaps it was time I began to do some thinking myself. I did—and that's why I'm on this train. I thought you might have been wondering."

"I'm still wondering how you ever got mixed up in it."

"It's the story of almost any Hollywood girl. Small town, small talent, a little beauty, foolish ego, blind ambition. In my case I varied it a little. I worked as a secretary in New York while I studied drama. I saved enough money to go to Hollywood. I had a new idea, I thought, of crashing the movies. I would work as a secretary and get in by the back door."

"That was smart."

"Except that a lot of others had the idea ahead of me. And the industry was saving money by letting out twenty-five-dollar secretaries. So I went to school again, thinking that was the best way of getting work somewhere. One day a man came and picked me out. He said he was a private broker. He outlined a position that was unusual, to say the least. His hobby was gambling, scientific gambling. He wanted somebody to keep the records for him. He also wanted somebody who would be presentable enough to accompany him to gambling clubs, to keep records of his play there. The job would pay forty dollars a week—and he would furnish the clothes necessary to go to such places."

"Huh." Terry's comment was eloquent.

"That's exactly what I thought; but he insisted that it would be a strict business proposition. He asked if I were interested in breaking into pictures."

"The old gag!"

"Except that this was a new approach. He said he played mostly at the Circle where I would mingle with the top-flight people in the industry: producers, directors, actors. Well, if you know your Hollywood girl, that is the irresistible temptation. She believes in her heart that all she needs to become a star is for the right man to see her."

"And you went for it."

"Not right away—there was one more requirement."

"There always is."

"Not what you think. It seems there is an old gambling tradition that it is lucky to sit next to a red-headed girl."

Terry grinned. "There might be something to that. You didn't bring me any bad luck."

"I hope not." She looked at him quizzically. "You know that in Hollywood, a thing must be phony to be good?"

"That's why I'm leaving the place."

"Can you stand a shock?" When he did not answer, her hands went to her gorgeous red hair. She gave a few tugs and the hair came off. Terry sat with open mouth, looking at the red hair in her hands, at the short, blue-black ringlets on her head. His face broke in a slow grin and he shook his head slowly. "Well, I'll be damned—a wig!"

"Transformation is the word."

"And the right word. Gosh—you don't even look the same. It does things to your face—and eyes. You're not the same girl at all."

"I hope you're right. I never really liked that girl with the red hair." She shook her head vigorously, ran her fingers through the black curls. "Do you mind if I leave the thing off for awhile? It's so comfortable without it."

"Go right ahead, relax, you're among friends." He picked up the transformation, examined it carefully. "I've heard about these things but I never saw one before."

She smiled. "You've seen plenty—but didn't know it."

"I can believe that. Know something funny? Just a little while ago I was sneaking a look at your hair to see if it were real. I mean if it were dyed—and decided it was on the level."

Her glance was affectionate. "Women probably take you for a ride on all sorts of things—you're the type."

"Hey—I don't like that. Dan said the same thing."

"I meant it as a compliment."

"Dan didn't." Their eyes met again, seriously. Terry said: "So you were working for Ramon?"

She nodded. "He asked if I would mind wearing a transformation. Well—it was a job and I decided to take a chance."

"Where does Johnny figure in this?"

"That's what still puzzles me. He began to be personally objectionable, but a girl gets used to that sort of thing after awhile in Hollywood—"

"I've noticed that." His tone was caustic.

"But I began to get a feeling there was something back of it all, something between Johnny and Ramon that I didn't understand, that they were using me. Even then I hung on, hoping for the right man to notice me."

"They must have noticed you plenty."

Her eyes dropped to her hand and there was a bitter note in her voice. "They noticed me—yes—but it was not until you looked at me last night that I admitted just what they saw." She glanced at the transformation. "Soon as I get off this train I'm going to take that thing off and try to forget that I ever wore it." She looked frankly at him, as if she had made a chastening but purifying confession. "Well, that's the story of another Hollywood girl.'

"Does Ramon know you're leaving?"

"Yes."

"Did he object?"

"Well, at first he seemed surprised when I told him I was thinking of it—then he agreed; in fact, it was he who advised that I leave so quickly. That sort of frightened me, and definitely made up my mind."

"When was this?"

"Last night—or this morning—when he brought me home. He asked me to come to the office this morning and pick up something he wanted delivered in New York. So I did—and here I am—and feeling very lucky, somehow, to be here."

Terry said: "You don't know how lucky you really are."

"Why do you say that?"

"There is something between Ramon and Johnny. I'm not sure what it is—but I know Dan didn't come out here just for a vacation.

You heard that talk at the table about a murder in Johnny's old place in New York? I've got an idea that Dan figures Ramon was mixed up in that, too."

She was agitated. "Did he say that?"

"He wouldn't talk about it—just told me to stay out of it."

"He's right. I'm sorry that you had to get in it at all because of me."

"I'm not—if it helped you get out. I think you're too fine a person to be mixed up with those rats."

Her fingers were racing again. She watched them. "What else did Dan say about Ramon?"

"Nothing much; but I'm sure he thinks there's a swindle somewhere. He said Ramon was Brooklyn white trash. He's not a Mex, is he?"

"I'm quite sure he isn't—but he's not a really bad person. I'd like you to know that. I mean—he was always nice to me."

"I'm glad to hear that."

She turned to him with a sudden, surprising intensity. "You don't belong in this. Promise me you won't do anything more?"

He laughed lightly. "But what could I do now? I'm not going back there. I'm out of it." He touched her hand. "And so are you. Be happy about it. So now let's forget it. Look at that sky."

Outside it was growing dark, somewhat ahead of schedule, because a great black cloud, with tattered, streaming edges, was reaching over the sky, shutting out the fading light.

She whispered: "It looks like Dracula's cloak."

They were silent, watching the sky.

Finally the train ran out from under the cloud and into a natural twilight, and they came to a brighter mood. The girl asked: "Why don't you ever let Hercules fall in love?"

"If Herky fell for every doll he saves, he would either be fickle or a bigamist—and the public wouldn't like it."

"Charlie McCarthy is fickle."

"But Herky is a different kind of a guy. His appeal is his sincerity. If I fool around with that, he loses his integrity. And integrity is the finest quality any person can have," he stopped, twanged his nose. "Maybe that's it."

"What's what?"

"What's been wrong with Herky. In Hollywood I've been holding my tongue in my cheek—formula—formula. So I don't believe it. So I do a machine job. So it don't ring true." He turned to her. "You might laugh at this—but when Herky is going good, I believe everything he does is right—"

"But you should. You're an artist."

He scoffed. "I'm just a guy that draws for the funny papers."

"When you make millions laugh or cry and feel—Terry—when you make them *feel*, you're an artist. If you want to make them feel Hercules, *you've got to be Hercules.*"

"Too many people think I'm Hercules now. Last night nobody at that table knew who Terry Moore was—not even you—but they all knew Hercules."

Her eyes, in the half dark, were brimming points of mirth. "Don't tell me you're *jealous*—"

"Well, how would you like to lose your identity to a piece of paper? You couldn't think yourself much of a guy, could you?"

She was laughing merrily. "But, darling, if they like him, they must like you. Everything in the creature must exist eminently in the creator. So says Aristotle—so says Aquinas—"

"And I say nuts. The public never studied philosophy."

"People call you Hercules only because you're so much like him—unconsciously, perhaps, but why not?" She leaned toward him, her knees together and her elbows on her knees. "I'll prove it to you. What does your Little Hercules always do? He comes upon the damsel in distress, rushes to her defense, defeats the Black Knight—and carries the maiden away on his swift and trusty charger. Right?

"Well, Hercules, what did you do last night? Can't you see it's the very same thing, with modern variations—the damsel in distress, the Black Knight, the rush to her defense—and what charger was ever so swift and trusty as this one we're riding now?"

CHAPTER V

He was unimpressed, deflated. "Just a comic strip figure. So that's the kind of a goof everybody thinks I am?"

"Nobody consciously does—I wouldn't have thought of it if we hadn't been talking—"

"Dan told me the same thing last night in a different way. He told me I was beginning to act like Herky. He told me to leave all the heroic stuff to the funny papers."

She looked out the window. "Dan warned you against me, didn't he?"

"Why should he have done that?"

"Because he's your friend, Terry. And he's right. I think I had better go!"

"No—please, Ruth." He caught her hand.

She was uncertain. "But it's dark—"

He laughed. "Where else can you go? What can you do?"

She smiled. "Well—it's dinner time."

"We'll eat here."

"Terry—really, I'm no good for you." She looked into his eyes.

"Why not let me decide that?"

"Because you're too damned nice a guy."

"Well, if you're going to swear at me—"

"Silly." She laughed and sat down, "All right—bring on that food. You'll think I'm a wolf—actually, I haven't eaten a thing today. I packed all night and this morning I had to rush to get to the office and make the train."

Terry rang for the waiter. He watched, with a slow smile, and she readjusted the transformation with a few deft movements. "I can't get over that thing. It sure makes you a different girl."

She touched up her face, became the gorgeous red-head again, seemed pleased at his masculine amazement. "I really shouldn't have let you in on this—now you are apt to start questioning everything a woman does—and that might make you very unhappy, sometime."

After dinner had come and gone, and they were alone once more, she removed the transformation. Terry looked at her searchingly. "I'm trying to analyze the changes black hair makes in you—your head seems smaller; the violet in your eyes becomes predominant; and the black curls give you a softer, I might say, a sweeter, personality—"

"Ah—" she warned, "that's Casanova talking—"

"No, it's just what I think. Your personality becomes less spectacular—you are no longer the actress, just a—"

"A secretary?"

"Well, yes."

"And which girl do you like best?"

"I like 'em both."

"Politician."

"Well, you're not going to catch me taking sides between two girls—even if they are the same."

Terry turned out the top lights. "I don't like bright lights in a room," he explained. The girl, curled up in a soft ball against the window, smiled down at the burning point of her cigarette. He thought that she had a warm color, like the end of her cigarette.

It was a very dark night. There was no moon and the window was a magic lantern screen over which flashed pictures of the night: flares from ghostly mountains; beams from lonely cars; lights from distant stars. Terry twisted the radio dials until the picture was scored with music.

"Here we are," he said, "all the comforts of home."

"Home." He couldn't see clearly, but he thought there must be a cynical curl to her lip. "Dear old Fifty-fourth Street." Then, "Does Luella have a nice home?"

"Very nice. You'd be surprised at the number of nice homes in Brooklyn. Her father's a judge—and not a bad skate, when the old lady—Luella's mother—isn't around."

She smiled again at the end of her cigarette. He was sitting in the armchair, his feet propped against the window, and he was puffing the big-bowled pipe.

"Too much smoke for you?" he asked.

It was too much smoke for anybody but she said no, that she liked smoke.

They whirled in dance time through the stars.

After awhile the girl's voice came softly: "All the world out there— and here we are spinning along in a little world all our own."

"Like it?"

"It's so peaceful."

"Let's buy it."

She did not bring Luella into this little world. Instead she reached toward him and very gently placed her hand in his. "Terry   "

"Uh-uh—"

"It seems to be one of those moments, doesn't it?"

"Guess it does."

He thought it would probably be all right to kiss her; but he was afraid she might just be grateful. A grateful kiss was better than none, but there was something demeaning about it. Then, a first kiss was a definite moment from which time went forward or backward. Maybe better not to spoil it. He wondered if she meant the kind of moment that came from nowhere, that went the same way, the kind you always remembered, the little miracle of a thousand complexities suddenly drawn to form. If she meant that kind of moment—

He shifted his chair until it was beside the divan. She seemed to tremble. He put his arm about her shoulder and dropped her head against his lapel. "You're all upset," he said with soothing authority, "and you need a little rest. Forget everything back there. Just remember you're safely out of it. Nobody there can hurt you now."

"I should go to my room—"

"Are you going to relax, or do I have to put you to sleep?"

She said with mock capitulation. "My, how masterful you are." But she crept closer to him. After awhile she spoke softly: "Terry, every so often, do you suddenly stop and look at yourself and ask yourself how you ever happened to be in such a strange place—and why?"

"Don't you like where you find yourself now?"

"Yes—but—"

"Then pipe down, before I clip you on the button."

"I wonder just how that would feel?"

"Don't tempt me."

"I'm still wondering."

"Okay—sister—you asked for it." He tapped her gently on the chin with his forefinger.

"You brute, she said sleepily, "now make it better."

He kissed her lightly on the button. In the quiet dark, she found his finger and pressed it against her lips. So he made her lips better, too.

And she wasn't just grateful.

She dropped her head against his coat again and worked her lovely body into a comfortable sleeping position. Terry's fingers automatically smoothed her forehead. For a long while he had no thoughts at all, only feelings. Gradually he buried his nose in her hair, which was thick and soft and as pleasant to be near as a bigger chrysanthemum than he had ever seen; he could imagine such a flower because he also was dropping off to sleep.

A plane droned overhead and fled swiftly by the speeding train.

Terry awoke after awhile, looked out at the few stars which had broken through the black, dwelt upon the odd current which had swept this girl into his arms. She was sleeping like an innocent babe. Her fingers had caught his and hung on tightly when he moved a little. He marveled at modern girls and their daring ways, at changing times and people. It was just about this hour the night before when they had first met. He had sharply affected her life in that little while. He suspected she had changed his; that two people who found it so easy to love would not easily give each other up.

Her face was much younger, her body was soft against him, he was conscious of the faint perfume which came from the girl herself and not from any flower. The first chapter might also be the last. There were many such and some had burned through the ages. Dante had never achieved even this intimacy with his deathless Beatrice. Nor had Terry Moore achieved so much with his Luella. Luella, with all her books, knew so little about the volume which was Terry; and he realized he had never gotten beyond Luella's hard cover. But Ruth knew, for instance, what made Hercules tick. He felt that he knew about Ruth— that he had known it from the time he had first set eyes on her—when everybody else thought she was a tramp. Life was a funny business.

Terry made the girl comfortable on the divan. His fingers touched her neck and she awoke with a start; but when she knew it was he, she smiled, turned her face from the dim light, wriggled her spine like a caterpillar until she found the proper position. Terry covered her with his topcoat, whispered: "I'm going out for a smoke. I'll be back in a little while."

She nodded sleepily without opening her eyes. He said: "You didn't hear a word I said." A soft smile told him she had heard. She caught his fingers, lifted them to her lips, pressed her lovely body against the back cushion. He felt that it might be like this if they were married.

He turned out the light and went to the club car. The radio was playing dance music. The bartender was shining glasses. One man was listening to the radio—a man who wore a black hat—Johnny Duke.

Terry's first impulse was to go back and warn the girl; but he went to the bar and ordered a barefoot Scotch. The bartender, a light-colored negro of obvious intelligence and some culture, did not get the barefoot. Terry explained willingly that barefoot meant straight. It gave him something to do while he was thinking. The bartender liked to talk, and that helped, too.

Terry went to a chair, sat down and picked up a magazine. He was breathing faster than he wished. He didn't feel so sure of himself as he had the night before. Dan wasn't here.

Johnny was waiting, like a dog before a rabbit hutch, deliberately high-pressuring Terry Moore into this kind of thought. Terry wondered how long Johnny—or Morgie—had waited for the night watchman at the Golden Pheasant. Dan had once said that Johnny liked to beat them insensible with his fists and then turn them over to Morgie and his neat job of cutting.

What had the night watchman, and how many others, thought about in their little hutches before they came out—or were forced out? Probably what Terry Moore was thinking now—thoughts that made their blood run flat, that turned their hearts into jelly and made their lungs swell to balloons.

Terry Moore smiled. That it should be he, of all mild people in the world, without an enemy until last night, who should be sitting in his little hutch, while a mad and cunning dog waited patiently for the flight of the scared white rabbit.

Now Johnny was coming toward him. Terry felt his right arm begin to tense and the knuckles shape themselves into a rock. His jaws tightened and his eyes began to narrow.

Johnny stopped before him. "How about a light?"

Terry lit a match and held it. Johnny looked at Terry's fingers. "Pretty good nerves."

"Why not?"

Johnny was offering his hand. Terry took it. Johnny was trying to crush Terry's fingers. Used to such pressure from Dan, Terry knew how to fight it.

Johnny's hard attitude broke down to good nature. "Hercules, you're okay. You've got guts. I like a guy with guts. I'll buy a drink."

"Thanks—but I'll just play this one."

Johnny ordered mineral water for himself and sat down.

"Left town suddenly, didn't you, Hercules?"

"I've had reservations for a week."

Johnny looked at his glass. "Too bad about Ramon."

"What about Ramon?"

"Now don't tell me you don't know what happened to our mutual friend?"

"I don't know what you're talking about."

"Where've you been all day?"

"In my room, working."

"Well, they found the Snake today with a knife in his back."

Terry felt that he should be looking into the horrible eyes of murder; believed that if Ramon were dead, Johnny Duke had killed him or ordered Morgie to do it; but Johnny was matter-of-fact. "And it looks very much as if another mutual friend of ours did it."

"Who?"

"The redhead."

"That couldn't be true."

"Why couldn't it?"

"I just don't believe it—that's all."

Johnny's laugh crackled through the car. "Fell for her hard, didn't you, Hercules? Well, you're not the first guy; but they've got the goods on her, all right. She was at Ramon's office at ten this morning—and that's the time he went bingo."

"Why should she want to kill him?"

"Now you're asking me something. Of course, he was a ladies' man—and there's that old gag about a woman scorned. But the police say she did it for another good reason. You see, he got away with about ten thousand dollars of my dough last night—and the cops haven't been able to turn it up."

"I still don't believe it."

"Well, your pal Dan does. The Snake was stabbed with a paper knife from her desk—and with her fingerprints on it. She was his secretary, you know."

"I didn't know."

"Well, I just thought I'd tip you off, as a pal—so you wouldn't have any more foolish notions about playing the shill for her."

"Thanks, Johnny, but how could I play the shill for her—even if I wanted to?"

"Because there's a pretty fair chance she's on this train."

"How could she be—if she killed him at ten this morning?"

"She could have planned it that way—and used the train for an alibi. She could have made it, all right."

Terry nodded. "I suppose she could have, at that." His grin was disarming. "I suppose you have an alibi, Johnny?"

"I always have an alibi." Johnny laughed again. "How about you, Hercules? Where were you between the hours of two and ten this morning?"

"I imagine Dan would vouch for me. He practically put me to bed last night."

"Well, he needn't have bothered. You made me mad for a minute—but then, when I cooled out, I figured you had fallen for the bimbo and lost your head. Used to be that way myself—but no more. Turn out the lights and they're all alike. If you're smart, you'll figure the same way. Take that the way I give it to you—as a pal."

"Thanks. Dan told me the same thing."

"Dan's been around—he knows. He's smart."

"I'm just wondering, Johnny, if you're being so smart."

Johnny turned quickly. "What do you mean?"

"Well, if it's a fair question, if this girl doesn't mean anything to you, why are you following her?"

"Who said I was following her?"

"Okay—but suppose she were on the train and you should meet her?"

"Listen, Hercules, I'm no copper. As far as I'm concerned, the Snake was overdue. Who happened to kill him or why is no particular business of mine."

"Nor mine, either, Johnny."

"Now you're being smart."

Terry arose. "Well, thanks for the tip. See you in the morning." He started to leave.

"Guess I'll go back myself."

There was nothing to do, Terry decided, but to go on. If Johnny were going back to check, if he found Ruth, he would just have to find her. Terry stopped at his door. "Good night, Johnny."

"Good night." Johnny hesitated.

"See you in the morning."

"See you in the morning."

Terry opened the door. The dim blue night light was lit. Terry kept his eyes on Johnny Duke and backed into the room.

The girl was gone. The room had been made up.

Terry sat on the bed. He was having a very unusual feeling—of elevators going up and down from his stomach to his heart.

He was satisfied that the girl had told him the truth; that she was innocent; that Johnny Duke had either killed or caused Ramon to be killed; that he had either framed the girl or was ruthlessly taking advantage of what would undoubtedly be damaging circumstantial evidence against her. Johnny was after the girl for some reason of his own.

The girl had not left soon enough. She was caught between the law and the law outside the law—the criminal code.

And Terry Moore was caught. His problem was simple enough—but terribly difficult for a person of his type. He could protect himself merely by doing nothing; he could help the girl only by involving himself. If he abandoned Ruth Allison he would lose his self-respect; if he helped her he might, conceivably, lose his life.

He lay down on the bed, looked out at the black landscape, until his head grew hot with thought.

He had no sister; but he thought of Luella in a spot like this. He thought of his mother. Then there came a peculiar memory of his grandmother, long dead.

His grandmother had been a firm believer in things like fairies and tokens and knocks at the door in the middle of the night. She had never turned a person away from her door because God might have sent that person to her for help. An angel, perhaps; or a poor soul from purgatory.

Terry felt that his grandmother was telling him not to turn an angel away from his door; if this were not true, why was he thinking of his grandmother? And having this particular thought.

There could be purgatory on this earth.

He got up, lit the light and wrote a note.

> Dear Ruth:
> Johnny Duke is on this train. He said that Ramon had been found dead today; that he had been stabbed by a paper knife on which fingerprints which he said were yours, had been found; that the time of death was fixed at ten o'clock this morning. From what you told me this looks awfully bad for you. I believe Johnny is looking for you for some reason of his own. I want you to know that I believe you are innocent, that Johnny or Morgie killed Ramon and that he is trying to frame you. He said the police are after you. This is his story, of course; but you'd better stay in your room. I would come now but I'm afraid he might be watching me. I didn't tell him you were on the train. I'll come to your room in the morning and we'll see what can be done. I think Dan will help us. Try to get some sleep. You may need it tomorrow.
>
> Terry.

He sealed the note and rang for the porter. The girl, the porter said, was in the next car. He would see that she got the note immediately. The porter was discreet.

Throughout the night Terry's thoughts went round with the car wheels. His thoughts were mice, riding the wheels like treadmills, to keep from being crushed.

He hadn't known Ramon Toros nor cared about him; but the man had seemed a friendly sort underneath; and it was a shock to think that any person who had been so handsome and alive last night, could be cold on a slab tonight. A little thing like a knife blade—and that was the end of a story. Such a little thing between life and death.

Once Terry was aware of an eerie feeling, of a three o'clock in the morning impression that somebody was outside his door. After awhile it was so strong that he got up, lit the light and opened the door.

The corridor was empty.

He went back to bed and raised the window shade. The train was coming into a town—a ghostly town in the dark. There were only a few shadowy figures on the platform—workmen who were seeing to the business of taking on water, filling up ice tanks, checking the equipment—routine safety requirements.

The station was part of a hotel—a railroad hotel typical of this line. The town was typical, too—low frame buildings, a single gas station, very few lights, shadowy mountains—a fine place for a murder, Terry thought.

He laughed at himself, turned on the light, got out of bed, lit a cigarette and did a few bending exercises.

It was daylight before he slept—and then he seemed to be awakened almost immediately.

The police were at his door.

CHAPTER VI

There were three men in the delegation. The train conductor looked petulant and annoyed, as if all this were a violation of the sacrosanct unction of extra fare. There was a railroad detective, a truculent beer-barrel sort of man who was even more outraged than the conductor.

Then there was the Chief of Police of the town where the train had stopped. He was heavy-set, more with fat than muscle; he was about forty-five, wore glasses and a Legion button in his lapel. He was a calm, almost placid man, smiling and apologetic.

Terry sat up in bed and frowned at the conductor. "Is this some of your Giant super-service?"

"Never mind the service," the railroad detective blurted. "We'll take care of that. You get ready to talk."

"About what?"

"I guess you don't know."

The Chief of Police grinned. "Take it easy, Charlie." Then he turned to Terry. "The train stops here only ten minutes. You answer us a few questions and go back to sleep."

"Maybe," Charlie said. "What is it you want to know?"

The Chief was suddenly professional. "Well, about the girl who was in here with you yesterday?"

"What about her?"

"That's what we want to know—what do you know about her?"

"Why?"

"Tell you that later."

"Come on," the railroad detective said, "hustle it up. Start talkin'."

"About what?" Terry didn't like the man's tone.

"About the girl."

"What about her?"

"You'll talk, mister, or—"

"Or what?"

The Chief was annoyed. "Better let me handle this, Charlie."

"Okay, Chief—but we've only got eight minutes."

"We had ten when you started," Terry said.

"Now see here, wise guy—"

The Chief put up his hand like a traffic cop. "Easy, Charlie. You're using the wrong tactics."

"You know the kind of tactics I'd use on a guy like this."

"This ain't no coal car," the Chief said.

"He's got you there, Charlie," Terry chuckled.

"I'd like to have you there." Charlie glared. "Chief, we ain't gettin' nowheres."

"How the hell we gonna get anywheres with you doin' all the talkin'?" The Chief was puffing at Charlie. His eyes were alight, his cheeks bellowed and he was looking from person to person. Terry could see that the Chief had a temper under his placidity and he was probably a tough guy when aroused, which was why he was Chief. Now he turned to Terry. "Better start talkin', kid, or I'll have to take you off."

Terry shook his head. "I stand on my constitutional rights. You're not coming into a man's room on The Giant, abusing him—"

"Who abused you?" Charlie demanded.

"You did—and I'll report you to the company."

"Come on," Charlie said. "Let's take him off."

Terry warned the conductor, "If anybody lays a finger on me—or my baggage—I'll sue the company."

The conductor glanced unhappily at the Chief, who merely shook his head. "It never come up before."

Terry said, "And I think I've got a good case right now."

"Nobody abused you," Charlie insisted.

The conductor was looking at the Chief. "Looks like you'll have to come along with us."

The Chief turned to Terry. "Come on, how about it, kid, give a guy a break. What about the girl? Did she do it—and where is she?"

Terry asked: "Did she do what?"

"See?" Charlie threw up his hands in disgust.

"Well," the Chief said, "looks like we go on."

"I'd take him off," Charlie insisted. "He's bluffin' about knowin' the law."

Terry said, "I've been around too long with Dan Colby not to know a few things about how public ignorance is taken advantage of by the cops."

"You mean Dan Colby—of New York?" The Chief was alert.

"I was with him all of Saturday night."

"You say—Saturday night?"

"That's right."

The conductor said: "Time's almost up, Chief."

"I'm going with you."

Terry smiled. "Be glad of your company, Chief. Do we need Charlie?"

"No, we don't have to have him."

Charlie objected. "What do you mean—you don't need Charlie?"

The Chief's temper was rising. "I got jurisdiction, ain't I?"

"Tryin' to grab the glory, uh?"

"You'll get your share of the glory. Now get outa here—and give the man a chance to get woke up so he can think."

The conductor had his hand on the door. "Come, Lieutenant," he said. "We've done our duty."

When the door was closed, the Chief glared at Terry for sympathetic confirmation. "Lieutenant! Huh. These railroad dicks. Trouble with Charlie, he always thinks he's pulling a guy off a coal car."

"When I made that crack about cops—you know who I meant, didn't you, Chief?"

"Sure—I know who you meant, all right."

"Have a cigarette?"

"I can't ever use 'em before breakfast. Funny—some guys like a smoke before breakfast. I never could."

"You mean you haven't had breakfast yet?"

"No. That Charlie got me up, too—so I know how you feel."

"How about breakfast with me?"

"Okay with me." The Chief got up. "I'm going to see that Charlie before he gets off to make sure he don't do nothin' foolish."

"What do you eat for breakfast, Chief?"

"Anything. Anything at all. There's nothing wrong with my appetite." The Chief's sudden laugh was like the blare of an accordion.

When he had gone, Terry rang for the porter. The big black's gaze was averted. "Porter—a menu—and a morning paper—quick."

"No papers this mornin'."

"What do you mean no papers this morning?"

"That's what the Chief say!"

"Oh. All right—bring the menu—and don't look at me that way. I haven't robbed a bank."

"Yes, sir."

"Porter—remember the girl who was in here yesterday—is she still on the train?"

"Cain't say, sir."

"All right—bring the menu."

Terry closed the door, annoyed. The man was actually acting as if Terry were already on the way to jail, instead of going under routine questioning. The girl was in a jam, all right. If he could get his hands on a paper he'd know better what to say.

Terry tried the radio but got nothing but exercises. The cheery voice of the instructor maddened him. Nobody but children ever got up so early feeling so fine. Terry was always dopey—particularly so this fine morning.

The porter cleared the room, so that, when breakfast came, Terry and the Chief sat by the window and watched the bright world go by. The top of the sky was a pinkish pate; around the lower edges there were white clouds. The sky looked like a bald head with a fringe of white hair.

The Chief was impressed. "This is the life," he chuckled. "The wife should see me now. Better turn that radio off."

"Don't you like music with your meals?"

"We can talk better," the Chief looked at his watch. "I don't want to go no further than I have to."

"We'll get along. I just didn't like Charlie barging in and getting tough. All right, what's it all about?"

"That girl you had dinner with last night—you spent a lot of time with her, didn't you?"

"All I could. You wouldn't blame me if you had seen her. By the way, I was supposed to have breakfast with her this morning. Suppose we invite her in. Wouldn't you like to meet her?"

"Hah." The Chief's accordion laugh bellowed and died to a wheeze. "Wouldn't I?" Then he looked suspiciously at Terry. "Might as well cut out the kiddin', Mr. Moore, and get down to cases."

"What cases?"

"Murder cases."

"What murder cases?"

"I suppose you don't know."

Terry cut his ham with the side of his fork, remembered that Luella didn't approve. "Listen, Chief, let's quit talking riddles."

The Chief smeared marmalade over a slice of toast. "Shoot the java."

Terry passed the coffee. "I was out Saturday night with Dan Colby. We got in about two o'clock. I was up at eight-thirty, on this train at eleven. I met a girl on the station. I invited her to my room. We sat around and talked and played the radio. We ate here—you can see how comfortable it is?"

"You're tellin' me."

"All right. Then we got to talking about the strip—"

"The what?" The Chief eyed him suspiciously.

"Comic strip—Little Hercules—ever heard of him?"

"He's in the funny papers."

"I put him there. I'm the fellow who draws him."

The Chief was properly impressed. "Okay—then what?"

"That's all. We talked until about eleven o'clock. The girl went to her room. I went to the bar and had a drink and came back here and went to bed."

"So that's your story, is it?"

"That's all. Now maybe you can tell me what it's all about. Has the girl done something she shouldn't—is she under arrest—or what?"

The Chief grinned. "How about that cigarette, huh?" He tapped the end, lit it, enjoyed the first whiff of smoke as if he were rolling it around his tongue. "Nothin' like that first inhale after breakfast. After dinner, I like a chew. After supper, a tobie. I'm a funny guy about tobacco. If I smoke before I go to bed, it keeps me up all the night."

"Sounds like ulcers," Terry offered.

"There's one thing you didn't mention," the Chief said, looking at the end of his cigarette.

"All right, ask me."

"Don't answer too quick. It might get you into a lot of trouble. So don't answer too quick. It's a yes-or-no answer—so take your time before you say anything."

"All right, only don't make it so mysterious."

"Did you know this girl before you saw her on the train?"

"No."

"Sure of that?"

"Now listen, Chief—"

"Okay. Yesterday a guy was found murdered in an office building in Hollywood—a guy named Ramon Toros—"

"I heard that—on the radio."

The Chief looked at the silent radio.

"Did you know this fella Toros?"

"I met him the night before, with Dan Colby."

"Was he winning money?"

"He was supposed to be on a streak. I won almost two grand myself that night."

"Got it with you?"

Terry opened his wallet and flashed the money. The Chief said: "Did you see this girl with him?"

Terry smiled.

"Don't try to trick me, Chief. I told you I never saw her before."

The Chief looked at his watch. "Plains City in fifteen minutes. Better get yourself packed."

"Why?"

"You're getting off."

Terry was shocked. "You can't do that, Chief."

"You're under arrest."

"On what grounds?"

"On grounds of harb'rin' a murderer, aidin', abettin' her escape."

Terry began to laugh. "That's silly. My newspaper syndicate will make you a laughingstock."

The Chief's eyes bellowed and so did his voice. "I've had about enough out of you. You're no more the guy what draws Little Hulks than I am—and I never drawed nothing but my breath."

"Okay, Chief—who am I?"

"You're a 'complice of this Ruth Allison. You admit being at the Cinema Circle Saturday night; you admit you knowed Ramon Toros. The girl knocked him off, grabbed the dough, and beat it to this train for an alibi, figurin' it was Sunday and he wouldn't be found till today. You kept track of things by this radio—and when the trail got hot you sent a note to her by the porter to beat it. She scrammed in the middle of the night with most of the dough. You kept two grand of it and had the guts to show it to me. Thought you were a cute guy, feedin' up my belly and givin' me soft soap. But you made your mistake when you showed me that dough. Thought you were kiddin' the hick cop, didn't you Well, thanks for the meal and get packin'."

Terry got packing.

CHAPTER VII

Plains City, before this surprising day, had meant nothing more to Terry Moore than a signboard at the railroad station which told how far it was to Chicago and Los Angeles. Now it had become a point of complete stoppage, at least until the phone call came through from Dan Colby. Terry walked about the office of the mayor, ignoring the collection of law enforcers who had gathered to give him all the doubtful flattery that attends the big-time crook caught in a small-time pasture. Their brown leather faces were eloquent with the belief that the phone call would completely expose him.

This thing he now saw in everybody's face annoyed Terry, impressed him, and finally made him very thoughtful.

He was being looked at as a *criminal*.

And he knew how it felt, for the first time in his life, to be deprived of what he now fully recognized as the most precious of all human privileges—liberty.

He began to understand faintly the psychological reaction of people branded with this intangible letter of guilt even before their guilt is proved. He thought it might be easy enough for a decent person who is told that he is of the criminal class, to begin to think and react, and, conceivably, finally act like a criminal, if honorable doors were shut against him long enough.

They had given him the trimmings—taken his baggage, kept him from reading newspapers, twisted his answers, made the phone call to Dan only on agreement that Terry would pay for it if Dan disavowed him. All this for him, who had done nothing at all, whose life had been turned sidewise on the mere assumption of all sorts of things by police, who would not even believe that he was Terry Moore. It was a bit frightening to be so caught, even though he knew that Dan would soon bail him out.

But how about Ruth Allison, who had nobody to front for her, against whom there was undoubtedly weighty suspicion, circumstantial though it might be? These fellows would have her on her way to the electric chair by now. No wonder she had run away in the middle of the night, if her choice was the police or Johnny Duke.

Terry stopped at a window to look at the people on the streets below. Life went on for them in the usual slow manner. They were not caged as adversaries to society; but Terry Moore was caged while the real anti-social animal, who had also been on that train, had been allowed to go on untouched, unquestioned—

The phone rang. Terry dashed for it—but the Chief held him back with the traffic cop gesture. The Chief was yelling into the mouthpiece as though he thought an extra effort was necessary to carry his voice all the way to Los Angeles.

"Hello—hello—Dan Colby—yeh—huh—this is Chief Davis of Sulphur Springs—what's that—yeh—this is Plains City, but I'm from Sulphur Springs,—yeh, well, look, I'm holding that guy Charlie wired about—you know, on that Toros murder out there—he was hiding the girl and helped her escape—I think he's in on it—he's got part of the dough—here's what I called you for—he keeps saying he knows you— says he's the guy who draws Little Her'kles in the funny papers— huh—The Giant—huh—well, you talk to him—"

The Chief turned to Terry who took the phone almost by force. "Hello, Dan—" Dan's laugh interrupted him.

Terry said: "I'm glad you think it's funny."

"Who got you out of jams before I took you to raise?"

"I didn't get in jams. Listen, tell these guys I didn't rob the treasury, will you—or blow up the City Hall—I'm Two-Gun Terry or something like that. They've got my baggage and my money and I'm not allowed to see any papers."

"Well, why didn't you tell them the truth?"

"I did tell them. And what did it get me? They build up a case against me I'd have to believe myself if I didn't know better. I'm not

Terry Moore but a crook. I helped knock off Ramon Toros and rob him; I kept track of developments with my portable radio; I'm still carrying part of the loot—"

Dan interrupted: "Okay, Sonny Boy, save that show for the cow cops—but don't try to kid your Uncle Dan. He knows better. You were surprised to see Ruth turn up on the train; she told you a fancy story to account for it; you went overboard for it as usual; she stayed close to your radio and hid out in your room, using you for a sap again, killing two birds with one stone. Then she ducked the train—and you're covering her up. Isn't that more like it?"

"Listen, Dan, I've heard enough of those landscaped theories to hold me for awhile—"

"We're wasting time, kid. We've got the dope on her. It's like I said before, leave the hero stuff to the guy in the funny papers and let's get down to business. A guy has been murdered—not a very nice guy—but still a guy. You're supposed to do your duty like any other good citizen in a time like this. If you had done that in the first place you wouldn't have been picked up. Now tell me everything she said."

"She said that what happened Saturday night made her see she was in a tough spot—so she talked it over with Ramon and he advised her to pull stakes. So she did—and that's all."

"But she didn't say anything about knocking Ramon off and going domino with his money?"

"Now you're talking like these cow cops—" Terry was conscious of a stiffening of the alert leather faces about him. "Now get this! I think the person who killed Ramon was on that train all right but it wasn't Ruth. I don't suppose you know—"

Dan interrupted. "I know all about that but we're not putting it out yet—so keep your lip buttoned. Now I happened to be the guy who found Ramon. He had called me to come in and see him. When I got there about noon he was bingo. I grabbed this other guy and brought him in right away. He had an alibi . . ."

"What does that prove?"

"In this case it was pretty good. Anyhow we turned him loose, figuring he might lead us to the girl."

"What does he want with her?"

"You figure that out. Anyhow, he flew to catch the train and that's how we knew the girl was on there. When Ramon was identified and she saw Johnny, she beat it. It all fits well enough."

"But it's all circumstantial."

"Well, unfortunately, Terry, these people who go about knocking off other people never set up cameras or microphones at the scene of the crime. So we have to do the best we can. Now here's what I want you to do—sit down and draw me a sketch of the redhead."

"Why?"

"Because we haven't been able to dig up a picture of her. She seems to have been very cagey about getting herself mugged—and she was a loner with other dolls, so there are none of those picnic shots with the candid cams."

"But I'm not a portrait artist—"

"That's all right—you're pretty good. Just make one as good on paper as you did of Johnny Duke on the tablecloth and it will be all right—those flaming tresses will do the rest."

"But I drew Johnny from life. I don't remember much about this girl—"

"Quit stallin', son, and get to work. You never spent ten minutes with anybody who attracted you without putting them down on paper."

"I don't think I should—"

"What you think doesn't mean anything this time."

"She didn't kill him, Dan—"

"Maybe she didn't, but she's in this up to her ears—or she wouldn't have done the Houdini. Now you quit talkin' and start drawin'—if you want out of that bird cage."

"Save that for the customers."

"What you don't seem to realize, Sonny Boy, is that you are one of my customers. You know me—if I catch my grandma on the other side of the street I just ain't got no grandma. So take your pick, pal."

"Carmichael would take the roof off this joint—and the hat off your head—think of all the publicity he could get out of this for Empire Features—"

"And he just might keep you in there for the same reason. But we're wasting time, kid. I know you're nuts about the doll—"

"I'm not—"

"Pass that. I can see why you don't want to put the finger on her; but this is a spot where you've got to show your colors, like any other good citizen. You can't afford to do anything else—there's your girl back in Brooklyn, your job—how would it look for the guy who draws Little Hercules, who is so strong for law and order, to be put in the position of obstructing justice—you've got to remember—"

As Dan went on with his persuasive arguments Terry remembered what he should have thought of long ago, what had been troubling his subconscious ever since Johnny Duke had first come on the train.

A man had been murdered; before the murder had been discovered, Terry Moore had put it into a comic strip—with the actual faces of the victim, the girl fugitive, of Johnny Duke, Morgie Stern, and Dan Colby. And Terry Moore would quickly be identified as Little Hercules.

He must stop publication—and in such a way as not to arouse Carmichael's curiosity. He could not do this by wire or telegram—because the police would be keeping a routine eye on him. Dan had allowed Johnny to run loose, hoping he would lead to the pretty fox; Dan was perfectly capable of using Terry for a hound. What the detective had said about his grandmother was true enough.

Terry must get out of here, hurry to New York. Yet the only way out was to give the police the sketch which would lead to the capture of the girl—

Then Terry Moore had one of his instinctive flashes. He interrupted Dan's persuasive oratory. "Okay, Dan—you'll have your drawing."

"Attaboy. I'll be in touch with you—lots of things I want to know—and, Terry, keep this other angle under the hat."

"You mean under the black hat?"

"You got it. And Terry—"

"Yeh?"

"Hustle that sketch—I want to make the afternoon papers with it—the farther she gets away, the tougher she'll be to catch. 'Bye, kid, see you soon. And one more thing—very important—don't talk to any more strange women."

"Nuts to you, pal."

Dan laughed. "Let me have that corn-crib Philo again."

As Terry drew the sketch of Ruth Allison, the police gathered round.

The facial characteristics were somewhat more blurred than Terry's usual style, but it was a very good sketch of a girl with red hair. Below the sketch Terry listed a description emphasizing the red hair.

Ruth, he assumed, would now be black-haired.

CHAPTER VIII

People no longer looked at Terry Moore as if he were an anti-social something to be caged; and he now could read newspapers, a hitherto unsuspected attribute of a free man. But as his train pulled out of Plain City, he wondered if the psychological stamp of the criminal had left its delicate imprint upon him.

He was conscious of an inner glee at having outwitted the cops; and he felt another reaction which he suspected might also be faintly criminal—the fact that he knew so much more about this crime than the newspapers. The press had, from long practice which Terry well understood, built up an imposing case against Ruth by putting their own theories into the mouths of authority with such handy phrases as "police say" or "police allege."

She had been Ramon's secretary; had been with him Saturday night; had checked out of her studio club hurriedly Sunday morning with light luggage, leaving two trunks of expensive clothing "to be called for." Her trail had led to the hideaway office at about the time fixed for Ramon's death; then to the train, assumedly with the money, and, after the identity of the murdered man had been discovered, into the night somewhere in the Rockies.

There was no mention of Johnny Duke beyond the fact that he was the owner of the Cinema Circle where Ramon had won the money which had now disappeared. The fact that Dan Colby was deliberately keeping Johnny's name out of it was significant.

Terry was amused at the manner in which the press was handling him. This was his first experience as a subject of news. The boys couldn't seem to make up their minds about him. He was variously described as a victim of circumstances, a chump, and a sinister fellow with a double life—and there was the whimsical suggestion that he was embroiled in the same sort of situation into which he had so often projected Little Hercules.

Terry understood well enough. This story was journalistic red meat and the tigers were tearing ravenously at the juicy steaks of murder, love, gambling, racketeers, Hollywood, Broadway, the beautiful girl fugitive and "the puzzling personality of Terry Moore." Ramon was dead, the girl missing—and since they did not yet know about Johnny Duke, the only live one about was Terry Moore. They were building him up as a straw man to kick around until they got their hands on something more substantial.

Terry had first thought Ruth's panic flight from the train, which seemed to be a confession of guilt, had been a mistake; but he was now convinced that she had done the wise thing. He still believed that the girl was an innocent victim of circumstances. The longer she remained at liberty the less chance police would have to make a goat of her; and the more opportunity Dan would have to nail Johnny Duke.

Terry must now decide his course of future action. Johnny Duke would know that Terry had lied to him about Ruth's presence on the train—but that was water under the bridge that would have to flow on. Terry's conscience was at ease. He had played fair with the girl. His immediate problem was to play fair with himself, to avoid unnecessary entanglements.

He turned to the problem of the strips he had sent on to Carmichael and the fact that these contained the actual faces of Ramon Toros, Ruth Allison, Johnny Duke, and Dan Colby. His imagination had been too realistic. If those were published, he would be under police suspicion; and Johnny Duke would be further enraged at this apparently deliberate attempt to connect him with the crime. The original strips must never appear; but to satisfy Carmichael, Terry would have to provide substitutes which would seem to be better than the originals. He realized it would be good business to capitalize the notoriety he had already gained by his accidental connection with the Toros murder. The gambling background was now better than ever. This was the break that Hercules needed, one that would not only recapture the clients who had canceled, but would probably add many more.

Terry went to work on a new series which would somewhat parallel the developments of the Toros case; but the new characters would be entirely fictional. Above all, there would be no facial resemblances to Ramon, Ruth, Johnny, or Dan.

It was late that night before he completed the substitute strips. He was completely exhausted and went to bed: but his sleep was troubled. Through his dreams passed Johnny Duke and Ramon Toros—and most of all the face and form of Ruth Allison, off in the dark, beating her way across country.

Terry awoke when the train was two hours out of Chicago. He went to the dining car, picked up a newspaper, prepared for the headline which would tell him that Ruth Allison had been captured. He was relieved to find that she was still at liberty; but nevertheless he got a series of jolts as a current of unexpected personal publicity charged through him. Page one of the *Chicago Star*, which carried the Empire Syndicate features was devoted almost entirely to Terry Moore and Little Hercules.

There was a large picture of himself, a posed still which he knew came from the studio syndicate. Under the photo was a caption:

LITTLE HERCULES IN PERSON

Across the bottom of the page was the Little Hercules strip of that day. It had nothing to do with the murder, of course, but was one of a previous series Terry had prepared in Hollywood. Little Hercules had made Page One, the first time any comic strip had achieved that honor, as far as Terry knew—because his master had become big news. He had pushed poor Ramon out of focus entirely.

The little Hercules in Person whimsy was apparently seriously advanced in the article written by Kenny Tompkins, ace reporter and radio commentator of Empire Syndicate. "Psychologists," Kenny wrote, with tongue-in-cheek, "are intrigued by the possibility that Terry Moore, after long association with his famous cartoon character, Little Hercules, has begun to think and act like his alter ego. By actually holding out on the police from an idealistic impulse, by risking his own freedom and safety to help an innocent girl, Terry Moore did in real life what he has been having Little Hercules do in person for the joy of 40,000,000 readers in 263 papers that use the feature from Empire Syndicate."

And so on.

Carmichael had done a good job. He had tied Little Hercules in with a murder mystery and had managed to get in a plug for Empire Features. Terry was sure now that he no longer had only the police and Johnny Duke to consider; he must also keep his left out for Carmichael, to whom Terry Moore was now just like any other name in the news, somebody to kick around for the glory of Empire. Even if Terry wound up in jail, Carmichael would not be worried. He could still draw in jail. Dan had been right about that.

In Chicago, Terry had his first brush with the press. He posed for pictures, reminded the boys that he was a newspaperman himself and understood their problem; but the trouble was, there was so little he could say. He had met the girl on the train they had put in some time together; they hadn't discussed her private affairs. He had expected to have breakfast with her the next morning. Instead, he had had breakfast with police who had routed him out of bed and taken him from the train.

No, he felt no resentment toward the police, even though they had delayed his return to New York. They had merely done what seemed to them the right thing. Terry admitted that the evidence against him might have looked damaging; but his friend Dan Colby had cleared that up by long distance. He had hesitated about giving the police the drawing of the red-haired girl. She hadn't seemed to him to be the type to be involved in a murder and he was reluctant to do anything that might injure her. He modestly pointed out that he wasn't at all certain the sketch would be of any help. He was, after all, not a portrait painter but only a fellow who drew pictures for the funny papers. The entire affair put him in an embarrassing spot; but there was nothing else he could do; and, anyhow, he was sure that the girl would be able to prove that the evidence against her was circumstantial.

It was obvious that the reporters liked the idea that Terry was a living embodiment of the knight errantry with which the newspaper profession cloaks itself. They wanted to know about Little Hercules, and Terry obliged by slipping them some of Luella's theories about hidden meanings, symbols, and a sense of justice.

Terry's entrance into New York was triumphal.

Photographers and reporters from all papers were waiting at Grand Central Station. Shutters began to snap. Reporters began to question, but Kenny Tompkins, who had come to meet Terry, cut them off. "You can read it all in the *Leader.*" Terry merely grinned and indicated that there was nothing he could do. He moved along in the vortex of newspaper people, curious passengers, and red caps, through the architectural barn of the station. Police made a passage through hundreds of people who swarmed at the train gate. Terry knew that he was merely the trained seal who was being paraded across the circus ring this day for the amusement of the populace. At the moment they were thumbs up—because his particular goofiness titillated them.

At the Empire Building, he was greeted by attendants as a returning hero. He went immediately to his artistic retreat which was one of several glass cubicles that flanked the corridor that led to the city room. The top half was glass, so that the sightseers who came through the building on hourly schedules with a guide, could see the "men who made Empire." The inhabitants of this section, privately labeled Murderers Row or the Goldfish of Empire, could achieve semi-privacy or protest against the proletariat, only by turning their backs. How they sat usually reflected the condition of their moods and egos.

Terry's place was dusty. Evidently the cleaning men did not read the front page of their own paper, which had announced the homecoming of "Little Hercules" in person. There was a stack of mail which had accumulated since he had left; most of it would be press agent literature which he still received from drowsy people who either didn't know he had left the sports department or just didn't care.

Terry was putting the place in order when the telephone rang. Carmichael wanted to see him. Terry took an envelope from his workcase and started for Carmichael's office. His route led through the city room. There he was a humorous sensation. They searched his vest pockets to see if Ruth Allison were hiding there; they wanted to know how Kansas jails compared with those in other sections of the country. Those who knew him well wanted to know how Luella was feeling these days. They wanted to know all the bright things which all the cute minds of the city room could think up. They asked him for autographs. Photographers retreated before him, making fake shots.

CHAPTER IX

Carmichael was on the small size, for a man; his shoulders were rounded from a lifetime over desks; he wore heavy spectacles, probably for the same reason. His head was snowy, and the top was bald. From the back he might have been seventy; but from the front, his age was cut to fifty-five by glaring black eyes, a cynical curl of lip, and the quick stridency of a cutting, impatient voice.

Terry Moore thought that, even from Carmichael's standards, he was performing nobly for Empire Features; he sought to prod the old man a little; "Well, what do you think of Little Hercules now—is he still gasping?"

Carmichael was in no mood to dispense flattery. He wanted to see the substitute strips.

Terry laid out the strips. "I've doped out a case patterned after this murder, Carmichael. I figured it would be great stuff to cash in on the publicity. So I've put Herky in an analogous situation, and have invented characters to go along—a girl, a detective, a gambling czar—"

Carmichael looked carefully at the strips with the expert eye of a connoisseur. Finally he pushed them away, fastened Terry Moore with baleful eyes. "This stuff stinks."

"Carmichael—there's a limit even to your bad temper." Terry, genuinely, surprisingly mad, stopped his own flow of speech.

"Well—did you go Hollywood!"

"No, I didn't go Hollywood. I bring you back something hot, and you start kicking it around—that's all."

"So you're bringing me back something hot. And that tripe's it." Carmichael spat on the expensive rug as if it were a city room wastebasket. "It's raining gold pieces and you're picking daisies—"

"Well, what did you expect?"

"I expected the real story of what happened—which even you knew was the story, because you sent part of it to me—before you started to invent. I want the continuation of that story in pictures just as it all happened. If you think I'm going to kill the biggest story I've ever had just to help you protect that girl—"

Terry cried: "You're going to kill that series because it's too good—because I imagined almost the exact murder before it happened."

Carmichael's bark was skeptical. Terry continued: "You wouldn't laugh so loud if you got a libel suit plastered on you—"

"You can't libel a gambler—he'd be afraid to sue—"

"Not if you accuse him of murder. And while we're on the subject, you may as well cut out all these goofy stories you've had Kenny Tompkins cook up about me being Little Hercules in person. You're not going to make a guinea pig out of me—and that's that."

Carmichael's black eyes were popping. "As long as you work for me, you'll do as I say."

"I don't have to work for you."

"You've got three more years on your contract."

"I'll go back to Hollywood."

"If you were any good you'd never have come back."

"If you're trying to make me believe you would black out the hottest thing in your syndicate, you must think I'm stupid. So let's stop yelling and get down to earth. The public will go for this series. After all, they only expect us to amuse them. We're not supposed to solve murder mysteries in comic strips."

Carmichael became quiet, more quiet than Terry Moore had ever seen him. He picked up the strips again, looked his oldest age.

"Sorry I lost my temper, Carmichael," Terry said. "But it's a raw spot with me. I'd gotten tired of hearing Dan Colby and Johnny Duke trying to tell me I was protecting Ruth Allison—and when you started in, it was too much."

Carmichael was quick: "What has Johnny Duke to do with this?"

"He has nothing to do with it. That's the point. I used him as a model for the gambler because it was at his Cinema Circle I got the idea. That was before there was a murder. If I used him in the strip now, it would look like I was accusing him. He'd be sore and I wouldn't blame him."

Carmichael rasped: "He wouldn't dare lay a finger on a newspaperman. If he did, I'd crucify him."

"That wouldn't help me any."

"Do you know what you're asking me to do? Kill the greatest story in the history of cartoons!"

"And you're asking me to take a chance on getting myself killed."

Carmichael spat again. "Don't try to fool me with that song and dance about being afraid of a gangster. You're welching on this thing because you're trying to help that tramp. She's guilty as hell and you know the story. You started to tell it like a good newspaperman should—then she got into you on the train. Well, you can't get away with it."

Terry was firm. "Get this, Carmichael. I don't think the girl is guilty. But that has nothing to do with my killing those strips. I don't know any more about this than you do; but I've already been tossed in jail and I didn't like it. I'm already public goof number one, thanks to you. I want to back away from this whole affair—but if you run those strips I'd be in it again up to my neck. Well, I think more of my neck than my ego—or your damned syndicate—and that's all there is to it."

Carmichael was unimpressed. "No guts."

Terry, stung, rose: "Call it that if you like—but I'm not going to be a hero for any organization that asks me to stick my neck out for circulation."

Surrender to rebellion did not come easy for Carmichael. He delivered an oration about old-time reporters and newspaper tradition. He all but wept over the necessity of giving up the greatest story of his career.

Terry let him talk, feeling that he was winning his point. Finally he agreed on a compromise Carmichael grudgingly proposed. Terry was to go on the syndicate radio station that evening as a guest of Kenny Tompkins and tell of his connection with the case.

Carmichael had a parting shot of sarcasm: "I'll have the microphone sprayed with perfume."

Terry said: "Take a spray at yourself."

After Terry Moore had gone, Carmichael called for his secretary: "Get me the file on Johnny Duke—and put in a call to the Los Angeles Office."

Terry Moore lived in a 20-story house that occupied an entire block on First Avenue, facing the East River. For convenience of the tenants, the building was technically divided into three parts, with separate addresses, lobbies, and elevators. The lobby of the middle house was as large as that of the average hotel, and had complete hotel facilities—newsstand, cigar counter, switchboard, telegraph station, ticket agency, barber shop, beauty salon, and small shops to serve emergency needs for both men and women. In the basement were rooms for servants and an outlet through a tunnel to the garage across the street where most of the tenants kept their cars. It was a little city in itself, in the heart of the big city, within convenient walking distance or a short taxi or trolley jaunt to Times Square.

It was only a few blocks from the Empire Building, which was why Terry had chosen the place. His apartment was on the top floor of one side of the buildings, with entrance through one of the small lobbies. Dan Colby had one of the terraced apartments on the center roof. Dan used the elevator in the main lobby; but he and Terry simplified their visits by using the stairway to the roof, which actually made their doors only a few minutes apart.

Terry's apartment was typical of the building—bedroom, bath and living-room, with kitchenette in one corner containing a small electric refrigerator, an electric grill, and a few dishes and pans. His trunk and golf clubs had arrived ahead of him. He did a preliminary job of unpacking, airing, and arranging the place, saw that the hardy flower he kept in the fire escape outside the living-room window was still toughly alive.

He took a good look at the East River, noted with a grim smile that the battlements of city prison on Welfare Island had never seemed so prominent before. Then he turned to the early afternoon papers.

Ruth was still free. There had been the usual clues and even a few false arrests of redheads from coast to coast—for it was now recognized that she might be anywhere within the country's borders. Terry felt that she would not be found; but he was beginning to weary of

Ruth Allison. In these normal surroundings again, Terry was beginning to agree with what seemed to be the majority opinion—that he did have something of Little Hercules in him after all.

The broadcast would wind it up. He would tell his story, make it plausible and harmless as possible, wash himself up with the dear old public—and if he never saw Ruth again it would be all right. She was exciting—but too much so—Terry wasn't geared for that pace.

He turned the radio in on WEMP, the station operated by his own syndicate, and lay down on the divan to think. Terry knew he was skating on thin ice. People didn't usually talk back to Carmichael for the well-advertised reason that once was usually enough.

Terry knew he was taking a chance on losing his job—but in this case there was nothing else to do. He feared that he had talked too much to Carmichael about Johnny Duke. There was such a thing as knowing too much about the wrong things. And he could see Johnny's viewpoint well enough. Terry had stuck his nose in Johnny's business dangerously!

He heard his name on the radio. The announcer was telling the public that Terry Moore, Little Hercules in person, would appear as guest with Kenny Tompkins that evening and give his own inside version of the Gambling Murder Case to the public for the first time. Sensational disclosures were hinted. Terry talked back to the announcer and the public—told the latter not to be fooled because they weren't going to hear a thing they didn't already know. He drifted into a radio sleep in which he was thoroughly relaxed, yet conscious of music and talk that came from the loud-speaker. The announcement about Little Hercules was given at frequent intervals. Each time Terry warned the audience not to be fooled because they weren't going to hear a thing they didn't already know.

He was roused by the telephone bell. A telegram was coming up. It was from Dan Colby.

FLYING IN TONIGHT KEEP THAT ANGLE UNDER
THE BLACK HAT KEEP PUNCHING

Terry felt much better. He told himself that this was why he was so insistent about keeping Johnny Duke out of the case. It would be comfortable to have Dan back in his corner. Of course, there was the business of the black hair and the red hair—but Dan would never know about that unless the girl told him.

Terry felt like a man who has been on a visit from his mind and to whom old ideas were gradually returning. One of these, he discovered, was a somewhat overweening recollection of Luella. It was four-thirty and she did not like him to call at the library but he suddenly had to know what she thought.

Her cool voice was friendly enough. "So you remembered me after all, Little Hercules?"

He hadn't expected this from Luella who didn't often go in for whimsy. He forced a laugh. "Well, I've been so busy with one thing or another on this business since I got in—it's been an awful headache—"

"All of it?" She was distinctly out of character. "Some of it must have been nice—from all reports."

"It's been a pain in the neck—like one of those bad dreams—I still can't understand it."

"I've had a little difficulty myself."

That was distinctly a crack. He explained: "The funny thing is that it all seemed simple and logical enough at the time."

Now there was a familiar metal in her voice:

"Sharp changes like that don't happen simply, Terry. There was, of course, fertility in you. You are the very type of man to do the things you've done and think them simple; the existence of Little Hercules is ample proof of that. But the reagent had to be powerful, to bridge the intangible between your alter ego and you."

"Please, Luella, don't you say that, too—"

But Luella was going in her best form: "I'm merely saying, Terry, that the attraction of this girl had to be almost explosively dynamic to have produced in you such a complete disregard for consequences. I can see that you don't yet seem to realize that a comparative stranger has upset your entire existence—without, according to your own testimony, half trying. That doesn't happen, Terry, unless there is a revolutionary appeal to some fundamental vital force."

He answered: "Oh—I'm not that dopey. I knew I was taking chances—but when I thought of a scared kid caught between the cops and the rackets, and still with enough guts to try to look out for herself and tell me to stay out of it, I just couldn't bring myself to make it any tougher on her."

"Do you still feel that way?"

"I don't think she's guilty—if that's what you mean."

"'Tell me, Terry—would you feel so strongly if she were a plain girl?"

"I hope you don't think I'm in love with her!"

Her laugh was clear and strong and her tone had something of that sadistic tone used by almost any woman in discussing another woman to a mutual man. "Poor Terry and his women—and your letters about how hard you were working."

He was nettled: "I suppose nothing I could say—"

"And why should you say anything? As you were quoted in the *Chicago Tribune*—or was it the *Mirror*—you are a single guy."

"I suppose anything I say would be used against me?"

"It probably would. It seems there is a powerful reagent working within me, too."

"Listen, Luella, let's have dinner tonight and talk it over. I'm sure I can make you understand."

"Sorry, Terry, but I have an engagement tonight—and, anyhow, I couldn't think of taking you away from your radio public."

"Luella—"

"Good-by, Little Hercules."

Terry had a lump in his throat, an empty-sleeve feeling about his heart—as if a long habit had been harshly amputated.

CHAPTER X

Ordinarily the Kenny Tompkins broadcast was a ten-minute stint in a small studio without an audience; but when groups of women began to gather at seven o'clock, an hour before time, J. G. Carson, privately known to his employees as the Emperor of Empire, ordered the program switched to the large music hall and extended Kenny's time. The studio was filled and the doors closed within a half hour. Disappointed women, loitering about the entrance to the building, attracted inevitable curiosity seekers. J. G. Carson took another look and had the world series loud-speakers hurriedly set up for the street crowds.

Terry Moore, walking into the fringe, asked a policeman what the shooting was all about.

The cop said: "All these goofy dolls have come to try to get a look at that dopey Hercules guy. They think he's some kind of a hero because he stuck his neck out for a dame. Well, let me tell you something: any guy who sticks his neck out for any dame, drunk or sober, black or white, innocent or guilty, is nuts—and this Hercules guy seems to be double nuts."

Terry was thinking along the same lines. He was sorry he had ever heard of Ruth Allison. He was nervous and frightened about this broadcast. He would go through with it because he had to; but he would use it to bail himself back to normality. After this night, Ruth would have to take care of herself.

He nodded soberly to the officer, circled the crowd, went to the back of the building and up the freight elevator to the broadcasting floor. There the full force of what he faced bit him hard. He realized that this was a coast-to-coast hookup and a lot of people would be listening in—Johnny, Ruth, Dan, Morgie, Carmichael—

One little slip might put him in deeper than ever.

Carmichael was a strangely happy churl. J. G. Carson was there, gracious with the excitement of a spectacular, unpremeditated success. He congratulated Terry as the miraculous author of this sensation. Terry, bewildered, said that he wished to hell that he wasn't, which J. G. fortunately interpreted as proper modesty and not the rebellious spirit which Carmichael's glance inferred.

Kenny Tompkins finally got Terry into the control booth where they worked out a rough idea of the interview. Terry pleaded with Kenny to hold him up, to be careful of his questions and to stop him if he started to say the wrong thing. Kenny patted him on the back, told him to get in there and fight, said he would be okay once he started talking, told him, above all, to forget there was a microphone there— and never to allow the thought of a nation-wide audience to enter his mind. Kenny gave him a stick of gum; and just before they were to go on, a glass of water and some cough drops. After all this, Terry felt calm as one of the condemned.

Now they were on the stage—Terry, Kenny, J. G. Carson, and Carmichael. The program opened with a musical signature, proceeded with the announcer, then a proud word from J. G. himself, who said that he regarded this event as one of the red-letter events in all the proud course of Empire.

As Kenny Tompkins opened his show, with a dramatic, dynamic, staccato delivery, Terry sat staring into the crowd, obsessed by the odd thought that two of those staring eyes and one of those indistinct faces must belong to Ruth Allison. She would be mad to do it; but there was a daring about her, a practical recklessness which might cause her to believe she was safest in a crowd, where least expected.

Terry had the horrible foreboding that he was going to expose Ruth Allison at this broadcast; but now Carmichael was nudging and Kenny was motioning and before he knew it, Terry was on his feet. Listening to the cheering women, he began to get the embarrassed feeling that he was the one man in a harem. When he showed this in his attitude, with a shy smile and jittery actions, a new hero was definitely born. All belief to the contrary, the man all women love most, is the man who becomes a boy before them; for all women are mothers, even to their lovers.

Kenny stemmed the applause, pointed to the mike, which had a powerful influence over the screaming crowd. He asked Terry if he were nervous and Terry said, quite sincerely. "Golly, yes," which was the right thing to say because "golly" was the word Little Hercules used in excitement. They liked his voice, too, because it was masculine but hesitant and not the dominating voice of a Mr. Know-it-All, which is how most wives see their husbands.

Terry, feeling suddenly at home, forgot the mike and told his prepared story simply, clearly, even humorously but with such sincerity that he was on the verge of believing all of it himself. When he had finished and was an assured success, Kenny Tompkins led the cheering—and then began to ask questions.

"Terry—what about this theory that you have been drawing Little Hercules so long you've begun to act like him?"

That drew a laugh. Kenny had his finger on the pulse of the crowd. But so did Terry. He grinned and answered: "You ought to know more about that than I, Kenny—I believe it's your theory." Even Carmichael got a laugh out of that—and J. G. was panicked.

"Now, Terry—or should I say Hercules—you've been looking out over all the beautiful women in this audience. I want to ask you one question: Do you see Ruth Allison out there?"

There was a hush. Terry answered: "No."

"Do you think you could see her if she were out there?"

"No." There was a titter and Terry amended: "The lights, of course, are blinding."

"Yes, sir," Kenny Tompkins said, "particularly when reflected by red hair."

The meaning of the answering roar was unmistakable. Terry Moore frowned.

Kenny continued. "Just what do you think of Ruth Allison?"

"I think she's a nice kid who got a tough break—and before this is all over, she will prove it."

"You really don't believe she had anything to do with this murder?"

"No more than you did."

"Do you think the murder will be solved?"

"I do. I think Dan Colby will pin it on the right man."

"Then you think it was a man?"

"I do."

There was a sibilant commotion over the room.

After the announcer had closed the program by suggesting that his listeners look for further details in the pink edition of the Leader, which would be on the streets almost immediately after the broadcast, the women rushed the platform for autographs. Terry wrote on proffered cards and books. He looked at each face, expecting that it might be that of Ruth Allison; and each woman took it as an expression of personal interest in herself.

The crush was becoming heavy and Terry was increasingly bewildered, signing his name, answering foolish questions, constantly smiling. Kenny Tompkins finally came to his aid with building guards, and took him back to the station office. Kenny was jubilant. He said this was his greatest broadcast, that it would give Winchell something to shoot at. Telegrams were coming in for Kenny Tompkins, Terry Moore, even for Little Hercules.

One of the wires was from Dan.

THANKS FOR THE PLUG BUT YOU TALKED TOO
MUCH SEE YOU TONIGHT YOUR PLACE

Kenny poured a drink, then began to angle around for the name of the man. Terry said: "I don't suspect anybody—that was just a slip."

"I see—nothing intentional?"

"No—and I didn't like that crack about red hair; and I don't like your stories about me and Little Hercules."

"You've got the wrong slant—you saw how those women went for you. J. G. was terrifically impressed."

"From the attitude around this shop you'd think the only thing in life is to impress J. G."

"You're working yourself up into quite a state, Hercules!"

"And don't call me Hercules!"

"You should be flattered. A newspaperman is very seldom news. I'm making you king of the cartoons. So don't be so damned fluttery. Have another drink."

"You wouldn't try to get a guy drunk and put the vacuum on?"

"Not on a brother newspaperman. I was just wondering about her. I've been looking up the files. A Ruth Allison had a couple of bit parts around here last year—but she had black hair."

"This one was red as a carrot."

"Women change their hair like we change shirts."

"I wouldn't know anything about that." Terry gulped the rest of his glass. "I'm going home and sleep for a week."

Kenny poured another drink. "Have another shot and you'll sleep for two weeks. I'm just wondering if the police are looking for the wrong-colored hair."

"She looked like a natural redhead to me—but why don't you run one of your famous lines—tip to the cops?

"It would also tip the girl, wouldn't it?"

"You're assuming she reads you."

"Everybody reads me, Hercules—I'm still the number one guy in this syndicate—even if I am fool enough to build you up as a contender."

Terry lifted his glass. "To the new champ."

Kenny drank—with his fingers crossed. He said: "You might give me a break in return."

"What?"

"Well, if she should get in touch with you—and anything comes up—let me have it?"

"If it's news you can have it. But I'm not expecting to hear from her—and I don't want to. All she's meant to me is trouble. I've been tossed in jail, threatened by gangsters and my real girl is sore at me. All I want from now on, Kenny, is to retire to a quiet, peaceful life."

A boy came into the office, left two copies of the pink edition,— just off the press. Kenny reached for the paper, swore violently, glared at Terry Moore. "So it was just a slip, eh? You might have given me the break on the air—"

Terry picked up the other paper.

Twin headlines hit him like twin shells:

LINK JOHNNY DUKE WITH TOROS MURDER
MAY REVIVE GOLDEN PHEASANT KILLING

CHAPTER XI

Beneath the headlines was a sketch of Johnny Duke in the black hat, with Terry Moore's signature in the corner. Under the picture was the beginning of the story, without a by-line:

> Last night, in concluding his sensational broadcast over WEMP, Little Hercules (Terry Moore) stunned a nation-wide audience by stating that a *MAN* had murdered Ramon Toros.
>
> This followed a flat declaration that he believed Ruth Allison innocent. Little Hercules did not name the man, but the *Leader*, on most reliable authority, has learned that the man he had in mind was Johnny Duke.
>
> A link with the unsolved Golden Pheasant murder has also been uncovered by the strong suspicion that Ramon Toros and Raymond Torrance, who furnished Johnny Duke's alibi in the Golden Pheasant case, were the same.
>
> (Story continued on next page)

Terry and Kenny Tompkins turned to the next page simultaneously.

> The *Leader's* informant points to the significant fact that Dan Colby, the New York detective who had been assigned to the unsolved Golden Pheasant case, suddenly went to Hollywood last week and immediately visited Johnny Duke's elaborate gambling casino.

Colby's arrival (this authority stated) led to certain sensational events now made public by the *Leader* for the first time. They began when Terry (Little Hercules) Moore, who had come to the place with Dan Colby, precipitated an argument with Johnny Duke over Ramon's secretary, the now famous Ruth Allison.

That night Toros was murdered and a large sum of money, which he had won from Johnny Duke, disappeared. The trail led to Ruth Allison on The Giant, where she had apparently hidden out most of the day by duping the same Terry Moore. The public knows the rest of the story—how the girl disappeared, how Moore was taken into custody, how he has insistently protected Ruth Allison.

What neither the public nor police know, however, is that Johnny Duke was also a passenger on The Giant —and is now in New York.

In the face of this evidence, police are now asking these questions:

1. Were "Ramon Toros," the habitué of Johnny Duke's Cinema Circle in Hollywood, and Raymond Torrance, habitué of Johnny Duke's Golden Pheasant in New York, the same?

2. If so, where was Johnny Duke—and his hatchet man, Big Morgie Stern—at the time of the two murders?

3. Is Ruth Allison merely a pawn, after all, as Little Hercules (Terry Moore) has insisted?

Kenny Tompkins was staring angrily at Terry Moore. "You could have given it to me for the air—"

Terry rushed from the room with the paper in his hand.

Carmichael seemed to have been waiting. He was sitting behind his desk, black eyes popping with intensity, when Terry Moore burst into the room with boiling violence. "Carmichael, if you were not an old man, I'd beat that bald head against your knees."

Carmichael reacted with porcupine swiftness. "They've been coming in here and telling me that for thirty-seven years—and none of them have done it yet."

"In all your thirty-seven years you've never pulled one like this before—you old vulture."

"They've called me that, too—but none of them ever said I wasn't a newspaperman."

"You can call yourself a newspaperman; well, I'll tell you what you are—you're a sadistic old ghoul who feeds off other people's troubles. A murder is meat for your crooked teeth. You stand there now grinning at me because you've put me in a hot box and I'm squirming— There ought to be a special kind of hell for people like you, Carmichael—on this earth—"

Carmichael was contemptuous when Terry's paroxysm crumbled from exhaustion. "You're like all the others, Moore—you come in here like a raging wolf and you wind up babbling like a school kid."

"Because you're such an infirm old hyena—"

"Whenever I need pity, Moore—you won't find me back of this desk."

"Carmichael, I told you I couldn't afford to be pulled into this thing any further. I told you I'd been threatened—and now you put me in the middle of a hot spot—"

"We're running a newspaper here—and we're supposed to employ men, not yellow-livered—"

"One more crack like that, Carmichael, and I'll—"

But Carmichael continued to rasp: "We're not going to lose out on a story like this for you or any other man. What's more—we're going to run those original strips you sent in—"

"You're not—"

"In two days they'll begin."

"I won't go on with them."

"You'll have to. When I've run those first three you'll be in such a jam you'll have to finish them to protect yourself. You'll have to explain how you knew so much about a murder before it was committed. I'd like to know about that myself."

"Are you hinting that I had anything to do with it?"

"I think this girl is in it up to her ears and you're in it somewhere. I don't care about that—but as long as you're working for me—"

"I'm not working for you."

Carmichael hesitated. "Is that a resignation?"

"It is."

"Then it's accepted."

"I'll take Hercules to another syndicate—"

Carmichael's laugh was cunning. "Have you read your contract lately, Moore?"

"Hercules belongs to me."

"Hercules belongs to Empire Features. We hired you to do it."

"It was my idea."

"Read your contract. I'm going to run the first three strips you gave me—then we'll get another man to go on with the strip. You go off pay in five days."

Terry Moore walked along the deserted streets toward his apartment. He had avoided the city room. For the first time in his life he had met up with a jangle of nerves. He wanted only to get to his apartment, have a quiet drink, and think.

The Big Show was over. The chief actor, Pagliacci, Hamlet, Hercules, or whatever he had been, was walking home. Nobody noticed him. This was New York, where all the great actors in all the great dramas could walk home alone in the dark; where Ruth Allison probably was; and Johnny Duke; and Morgie. Dan was coming. Everybody would be here, as if called for a final scene, the scene which Terry felt gathering in his mind, in his stomach and around his heart.

Everybody was here but Ramon. Ramon must have been buried by now. But everybody had forgotten Ramon—except Carmichael and some few little people who quietly mourned. It must be tougher, Terry thought, to mourn a man who had been murdered.

The desk clerk wanted to talk about the broadcast; but Terry cut him short. "Anybody call for me tonight?"

"There were some calls earlier—but no messages."

"If anybody inquires for my apartment number, don't give it out. I'm expecting Dan Colby—just send him up when he comes. If there are any more calls, give me a buzz first."

"Okay, Hercules."

Terry smiled. He had made a lot of fuss about being called Hercules—but he was going to miss the little guy.

Things were happening fast. In a few hours he had lost the two people upon whom his future had been anchored—Luella and Little Hercules. He could not believe that Luella would not come back. He realized that he had given her very good reason for feeling as she did; but he felt that, once he had gotten out from under the situation, and she had cooled off, they could work it out, Little Hercules, however, was something else. Terry would see a lawyer in the morning and find out where he stood; but he feared that Carmichael would have the law with him.

He supposed that he could go to work for another syndicate; they would probably ask him to create a similar character. But lightning didn't strike in the same place twice. The success of any myth was seldom the result of conscious planning; instead, it came from the harmonious clicking of certain intangible qualities.

Life would be very queer without the Little Guy.

All of this had been caused by a girl he hardly knew. Yet he could not really blame Ruth Allison. She hadn't come into his life—he had crashed into hers. She had even pleaded with him to stay out. It was even possible that she may have fled the train because she did not want him to become further involved.

As Terry left the elevator, he was relieved to find that the corridor was empty. He admitted now that he had been fearful that either Johnny Duke or Morgie might have been lurking in the homeward shadows. He could not blame Johnny for believing that Terry Moore had not only deliberately involved him in the Toros murder but had gone to the trouble of reviving the Golden Pheasant case. The news story in the *Leader* had given that impression. It was comforting to be back in his own apartment where he would have time to think his way quietly through the new problems which had come into his life. Dan's plane would probably be landing at Newark about now. Terry was inclined to tell Dan everything that he knew and let the detective take it over. This was emphatically not Terry's racket.

He went into his apartment, closed the door, and switched on the light. Johnny Duke was sitting in the big chair near the telephone.

CHAPTER XII

Johnny Duke sat like a heavy dark bird of ill-omen. His suit was of black feathery material and he wore his black hat. From his heavy head, which sat closer than ever upon the wide shoulders, his eyes, like unhappy thoughts, stared at Terry Moore with unrelenting malice. His voice was caustically calm. "I thought it was about time we had a little talk—a little personal talk."

Terry quietly filled his pipe, put the pouch and matches on the table near the telephone. He crossed to a chair by the door. He tried to keep his voice steady. "How did you get in here?"

"Nobody saw me come in and nobody will see me go out."

Terry saw the moldy, sliding eyes, saw the skin squirm over Johnny's bony forehead. When he did not answer, Johnny spoke again. "I couldn't figure out before whether you had guts or were just plain dumb. Well, you're just plain dumb."

Terry said: "If you're talking about that newspaper story, I didn't have anything to do with it."

Johnny's eyes were like the water of a swamp, gray-black and muckish. "And I suppose you didn't draw my picture for the front page?"

"They got that from a strip I had drawn. I didn't know they were going to use it."

"So you put me in a strip, too."

"I tried to cancel the strip but the paper double-crossed me. I just quit my job over it. You can call up and check that, if you don't believe me."

"So I can call up, can I?" Johnny's anger was rising. "On that broadcast tonight you went out of your way to put me on the spot—"

"That was a slip."

"They don't have slips on broadcasts. You had that all worked out with Tompkins. You had the newspaper story all set—it was on the street right after the broadcast. Guys have been killed for doing less than you've done."

"I don't doubt that."

Johnny started to rise in his chair. Terry checked him. "If you have any ideas, you might as well know that Dan Colby is on his way here now."

Johnny snorted. "He's on the Coast."

"He flew in here tonight. Now listen, Johnny—I don't blame you for feeling as you do. I guess I have stuck my nose in your business but I never intended to."

"Then why are you going down the line for this bimbo?"

"I never saw her until that night in your place. I popped off when I shouldn't have—I'll admit that; I just happened to meet her on the train. From what she told me, I thought she was all right. When I found out about that murder, I did give her some protection. I did lie to you—as far as I could see she was just a girl in a tough spot."

Johnny swore. "I'm beginning to believe there is something to this theory about your being like that little guy you draw."

Terry said: "If you'll sit back and listen, I'll tell you everything that happened. I want to get this straightened out. Maybe there is a Little Hercules in me—I don't know; but I'm not fool enough to go out of my way to look for trouble with you."

"I'm listening."

"Well, when I left Hollywood I had to do a new strip. I decided to do a new series with gambling as a background. What happened at your place seemed to be a good situation to start with. I drew three strips. I used your face, Ruth Allison's, Ramon's, Dan's—and I put Hercules into the middle of that."

"What was the idea of using real faces?"

"That's a trick of the business. Newspaper cartoonists usually have to work fast; we keep a lot of real pictures of people and scenes. To save time, we usually copy from them. I certainly wouldn't have used real faces if I had known there was going to be a real murder—"

Johnny snapped: "I suppose you just imagined it."

"I heard on the radio that day that a man had been found murdered in an office building in Hollywood, but that he hadn't been
identified. It seemed to fit. I sent those strips off before I met the girl
on the train or before I knew you were on the train. When I found out
about the murder, I wired my boss I was bringing in some substitutes;
but he suspected what had happened and refused to use them. He was
going to use the originals. I told him that it would put me in a tough
spot with the police and you. I threatened to quit and we compro-
mised on the broadcast. What I intended to do at the broadcast was to
get out from under the whole thing. Then Tompkins began to kid me
over the air and made me mad. I didn't intend to say that I thought a
man had done the murder. That slipped."

"How about the newspaper story? I suppose you can explain that
away, too?"

"The only thing I can figure is that Carmichael—that's my boss's
name—put two and two together and implicated you; then he called
Los Angeles and found out from somebody about what had happened
at your place that night. There were a lot of people there and talk gets
around. I certainly didn't tell anybody about it because that would
have implicated me. Carmichael had been working on the story; when
I made the slip over the radio, all he had to do was write a few new
paragraphs and rush them into print. If you know anything about the
newspaper business, you will know that that can be done quickly. You
know how soon a paper is on the street after a big fight. I went to Carmichael, told him he had put me in the middle of you and the cops. I
quit my job. That's the story. You can check on it."

Johnny looked piercingly at Terry Moore. "How much of that can
I believe?"

"All of it. And I hope you do believe it. As I said before, I'm not
fool enough to go out of my way to get into jam either with you or the
cops."

Johnny seemed to come to a decision. His voice and manner lost
hostility. "All right, Hercules, let's lay it on the line. Let's say you just
stumbled into this thing; let's say you have just enough of Little Hercules in you to make you do what you've done. Now I'll say this: I don't
want to have to crack down on you—for obvious reasons which you've
been counting on—Dan's your pal, you're in the newspaper racket—

there's no percentage in my running into either of them unless I have to. Now, if I can convince you that I've nothing to do with Ramon being knocked off and that she did—will you get out and stay out?"

Terry smiled. "I'd be crazy not to, wouldn't I? But it will be hard for me to believe that girl would kill a man for money."

Johnny was annoyed: "Why, you fool, she had the money with her on the train."

"How do you know?"

"He—" Johnny checked himself. "I know it. Why do you suppose I'm after her? Why do you suppose I want to find her ahead of the cops?"

"Why are you so interested in the money?"

"Because it's mine—eight thousand dollars—mine. Nobody's going to take that kind of money from me and get away with it."

"But I thought he won it from you?"

"He never won a dime from me in his life. He was a shill, a come-on for the suckers. I paid him a salary. He always gave the money back—until this time."

"What happened this time?"

"He didn't have a chance. She killed him with a paper knife in their office. She planned it to make her getaway on that train. She tried to throw it onto me. I was waiting for him to bring back that money—and Dan called me in. That was the first I knew he was dead. That's why I'm following her. That's why I would never kill him, you fool. He made money for me."

"Does Dan know that?"

"Sure."

"What was Ramon going to tell Dan?"

Johnny's head came up from his shoulders with a sharp gesture, with eyes that drove a steel of fear straight down into Terry Moore's belly. "What could he tell him?"

"I don't know. It just seemed to me—that night at your place—that he had it in his mind to tell Dan something."

"What would that prove? He was a cheating louse—a liar. So was your girl friend. They both cheated me. She worked for me, too."

"She told me she worked for Ramon."

"Oh, she did—and what else did she tell you?"

Terry's instincts warned him that Johnny Duke was near the edge of one of his insanities. Johnny was a little dancy, Dan had phrased it, about two things—women and money.

Terry said: "She didn't tell me anything."

"Then she didn't tell you about the package the Snake gave her that morning?"

"How could you know about that—unless—" Terry checked his speech.

Johnny was advancing toward him, slowly. Now his voice was low and swift. "What were you going to say, Hercules?"

"Nothing—nothing at all."

"It had better be nothing. Now get this. If you ever—"

The phone was ringing. Terry started for the table.

"Get away from that phone."

"Better take it easy, Johnny—that's Dan."

"Let it ring. You're not home." The moldy glare came into his eyes. "I didn't swallow that guff about Dan coming in; but if you ever tell Dan Colby—" He, caught Terry by the lapels, jerked him forward, tightened the lapels with one hand, slapped Terry Moore's face on both sides.

Terry's head was ringing, his cheeks burning. Nothing like this had ever happened to him. He reached for the telephone, knocked it to the floor.

Johnny slapped him again. "Maybe this will teach—"

Terry's humiliation became rage. He forgot that the man was Johnny Duke. His right fist cut across Johnny Duke's eye and nose. "Get your hands off me, you lousy racketeer."

Johnny relaxed his grip, snorted with bull surprise.

Terry waited, hands up in a boxing attitude long forgotten. His right arm was cocked to his shoulder. Johnny moved forward, feinting and jabbing as at a ring foe. Terry backed cautiously, alert, eyes on Johnny Duke's, a strange, sweet fury in his soul. Johnny's left hook caught Terry's cheek, caused a clanging of bells in his ears—Terry's right shot sharply again—landed on Johnny's nose. Johnny was on him with a flailing of fists, a wild fury that forgot science, with a weight that was too much for Terry Moore, who went down, realizing as he did that it was fatal to go down, that he might never get up—that his picture might be on the front page tomorrow as Ramon's had been—

Johnny was grunting and gurgling in Terry's ear. Terry felt the hot breath of murder on his face.

CHAPTER XIII

Terry first heard the buzzer, then a banging and shouting outside the door. As he cried out in answer, Johnny Duke scrambled to his feet, punching at Terry who hung on as he hadn't done since football days. The door opened and Dan Colby was on Johnny with a tiger leap, pinning him against the wall. Dan's partner, Tommy Donati, quietly closed the door. Terry dabbed at a bleeding lip.

There was a moment of tableau, of very little motion. Then Dan made a quick frisk of Johnny Duke, who was making cautious, exploratory gestures in the region of his left eye. Dan Colby's laugh was like a roar in a closed cage. "Looks like it's going to be pretty bad, John— I would say about a half pound of beefsteak would help a lot."

"We can get along without the wit and humor department." Johnny was recovering his poise.

"The boys will sure be surprised, John; I guess they will figure that a year of Hollywood softened you up. I never would have believed it, if I hadn't seen it with my own eyes. Well, let's all us sorority girls talk this thing over. Tommy, suppose you sit between these two, so John will be safe."

Tommy Donati grinned, took the indicated chair. He was tall, quiet, well dressed and good looking—much more of the young broker than the young detective type. He and Dan formed a team that was feared and respected along the rowdy Rialto.

This was a situation which appealed to Dan's sense of humor. He walked around the room slowly. Every so often he looked at Johnny's eye and sympathetically shook his head. Johnny had returned to a mood which was superficially amiable. Dan said to him: "Okay, John— dialogue."

"I just came here to have a little talk with this boy. Dan. I can't make him out at all. I met him on the train coming east and we had what I thought was a get-together talk. I went out of my way to be nice to him—thought we understood each other. Well, you heard the broadcast, I suppose, and you saw the newspapers. So I just thought I would drop up for a little personal talk."

"And then he slugged you?"

Johnny Duke grinned. "Well, you saw it yourself, didn't you?"

Dan turned to Terry with mock reproof. "I don't know what I'm going to do with you, young fellow. Johnny's a peaceful citizen, a big business man, one of our leading pillars of the community. You know, we just can't stand for people like you picking on people who just want to mind their own business. Now, what's your defense, if any? I heard the broadcast on the plane and I have seen the *Leader*. How come?" There was a serious note under Dan's fooling.

"I didn't want to go on that broadcast but I was forced into it. I was trying to get out from under this whole business. Tompkins tricked me into making that slip on the radio and then Carmichael double-crossed me by using that news story and giving the impression that the information came from me. I quit my job tonight on account of it." Terry glared at Johnny Duke. "I tried to tell this guy all that but he wouldn't listen. He was going to take care of me like he did Ramon and that night watchman—"

"I never said that." Johnny Duke was on his feet, livid.

Dan cried sharply: "Did he say that? Did he?"

"He didn't exactly say it—but that's what was in his mind. He warned me not to talk to you. Well, I'm talking. If you want to know what I think, that news story was right. I think he and Morgie did go to Ramon's office that morning to kill him and pin it on Ruth."

Dan interrupted. "Well, you're wrong about that. I told you before I had checked their alibis."

"I can still have my own opinion."

"So can I," Johnny rasped. "Since we're turning stool pigeon here, let me tell you, Dan, that your pal, here, whom you're always so anxious to go to bat for, has been giving you the cross since the thing began. He drew a better picture of me on a tablecloth than he did of her on paper. He hid her away on the train all day—why didn't he let you know she was there, if he was such a pal?"

"Because," Terry said, "I didn't know then there had been a murder—"

"That's a lie. I told you myself. You ran back to warn her and get her off the train—why didn't you tip Dan off then?"

Dan said: "That's a fair question, Terry."

"Because I had no idea you were looking for her. She had told me a straight story—she had told me why she had left. She had even told me she was at Ramon's office that morning before train time—"

Johnny's cry was exultant—"There's proof, Dan—"

Terry was swallowing. Dan was watching Terry. "What did she say she was doing at the office, Terry?"

"She said that Ramon had asked her to pick up a letter he wanted delivered back East—"

"Hah!" Johnny was on his feet. "The money—my money—she knocked him off and took my money—just like I told you, Dan—"

Dan asked Terry: "Did you see the letter?"

"No—I didn't pay any attention to it at the time. That was when I first met her on the train—before I knew anything was wrong."

"Why didn't you ask about it when you found out Ramon was dead?"

"I haven't seen her since then. When I went back to my room, she was gone."

"And why was she gone?" Johnny cried.

"Probably because she was scared to death of you. And now, I'd like to know a few things. How did you know she was on the train?"

"When Ramon didn't turn up with the money I sent Morgie to look for him. He saw her come out of the building—and he tracked her to the train—"

Terry pressed on: "And how did you know Ramon had given her a letter—if he hadn't told you—"

Johnny's eye slanted at Dan. "I didn't know. That's her story to cover up the fact that she killed him and stole the money—"

"And how come Ramon was knocked off just when he was getting ready to tell Dan something? And why, when I suggested that to you before, did you jump a foot high?"

Johnny's laugh was a sneer. "Who are you to put the vacuum on anybody? In the first place, you knew Ruth before you came to my place that night—why? Because she was tipping you off on how to win at my tables. I was watching. That's why you were so quick to get tough when I caught you—to cover up. Then the two of you got together, knocked him over, lammed with the dough—and since then you've been trying to protect her and pin it on me."

Dan glanced at his partner, then he said: "Well, it's been interesting to listen to you two boys playing detective; but we've got other things to do, so we'll call it a draw. You're both barking up the wrong tree. Johnny, the kid here has not been putting you on the spot—it's a guy named Carmichael, his boss, who's been handing him the cross right along. But I wouldn't pick on Carmichael or he'll have some of those gorilla truck drivers beatin' you with ball bats."

Dan turned to Terry. "And neither Johnny nor Morgie knocked Ramon off. I told you right after it happened that Johnny's alibi was okay. Johnny came here because he was burned about the Golden Pheasant publicity. Once the press starts to work on a thing like that, everybody gets excited and the cops make it tough on a guy in Johnny's spot." He turned to Johnny Duke. "I'll quiet that down—but I wouldn't leave town, John—and I wouldn't pay any more visits to the kid, here. Beefsteak is expensive. Anyhow, I'm taking over now."

After Johnny Duke had gone, Terry protested: "Why did you let him get away? Why did you stop me when I was pinning him down?"

"Because, as usual, you were talking too much. But now, let's all us girls sit down around the camp fire—and you can spill your guts completely." He grinned at Terry. "Slugger—you amaze me."

Dan interrupted frequently as Terry told his story—completely, except for the detail of the red wig. The detective was particularly inquisitive about Ruth's explanation of why she had so hurriedly left town; about Johnny Duke's various actions and reactions, and the inferential admissions Terry had seemed to detect during his conversation with Johnny.

He was sympathetic about Terry's job; but Terry was vindictive. "I wouldn't work for that old vulture again if they gave me the syndicate. He put me in the middle with you and Johnny, he practically forced me to resign—and now he says Hercules belongs to them."

"Does he?"

"I don't know. I'll have to look into that—but it gives you an idea of the gratitude of newspapers."

Dan watched the smoke circle from the end of his cigarette. "Well, kid, it's only been a few days since you told me how you had your life all charted. Now you've lost your job, you might have lost your life—"

"Believe it or not, I was saying my prayers."

"And how's the Brooklyn department?"

"Not so good."

"Old man Carmichael is evidently a louse—but he has had a little help in scrambling your eggs. I'm just wondering how you feel about the angel with red hair by now."

"I still don't see how I could have done much different than what I did—particularly after I had sent in those strips from the train. And I still don't think she killed Ramon—and I don't think you think so, either."

Dan began to walk. "What do you say, Tommy, we play we're detectives and do a little recapitulation, like they always do around page 247 in the books?"

"Okay. There are a few angles I'm interested in."

"But how about the boy scout, here? Is he a member in good standing of the Detectives' Union?"

"Huh!" Terry scoffed. "I've been the best detective on this case. I'm the only one who has seen the girl, for instance—"

"Touché!" Tommy chuckled.

"I've placed Morgie at the scene of the crime—and I almost trapped Johnny into admitting that Ramon told him the girl had gone with the money."

Dan stopped in the middle of a panther tread. "But why should Ramon have told Johnny that?"

Tommy asked, "Why did Ramon want to talk to you?"

"Might be something to that." Dan hesitated, then said: "Okay—let's see how it stacks up." Terry listened attentively. He knew that

Dan was checking, fitting in the new parts as he reconstructed the story. It went back, Dan said, to the Golden Pheasant when the night watchman was murdered.

CHAPTER XIV

"The watchman was an old guy," Dan said, "and he was beat up and cut up. It looked like a job Johnny and Morgie might have co-operated on; but they had an alibi, provided by this small-timer Raymond Torrance. As far as we could get, he was not a regular but just a fellow who dropped in every week and liked to play the half-dollar slots—and now and then roulette—and did pretty good with them in a minor league way. The fact that he was an occasional made the alibi stand up pretty well, although it always smelled of herring to me."

The crime was unsolved, they put the axes to Johnny's place and told him not to open up elsewhere. The Dewey exodus was on, anyhow, and Johnny turned up on the West Coast.

"Then, about a month ago," Dan said, "I am looking at a fan magazine and I read a piece about the Cinema Circle being the lush palace. I see a picture of old friend John as mine host; and I see a lot of movie big shots hanging around the tables; and I also see a picture of Ramon Toros, the rising cinema cabalyerro. Maybe it was the name or something about the face—anyhow, the coincidence of him and John together was too much. So I look up Raymond Torrance in New York, and he is vamoose, as they say in old Mehico. Furthermore, to me, he has always been a little to the lobster side because I could never find any of his kin. So I take a little trip to Hollywood—which," he grinned at Terry, "was where you came in."

"And you move me in with the nice people."

Dan chuckled to Tommy. "I wanted a good strong man with me, Tommy,—a guy who could fight his way—not having you along. Well, he started to tear up the joint right off. First he falls for Johnny's girl

101

and gets mad when Johnny musses her hair up; so he ups from there and goes to the bar and picks up this Punch'n Judy bag and I drag him out of that just as he is ready to denounce Elmer Mitchwin, the big producer, no less. Then we go to the tables and he takes two of Johnny's G's just like that—and bawls the livin' jeepers out of Johnny in his own joint. I finally get him home and he sneaks out, according to common report, knocks off poor Ramon, scrams with the dough, hides out with the doll, gives the cow cops the circulars and gets incarcerated. Uncle Dan to the rescue again. Then he becomes a helluva hero with the dolls—turns national broadcaster and we come in to find him beatin' the jeepers out of poor Johnny Duke who is runnin' like a thief for the window—window—" Dan turned to Terry. "How did he get in?"

"He was here when I came in."

Dan nodded. "Fire escape—same old stunt. Now a few more things to fill in. When I saw Ramon at the Circle that night Johnny gives me the Mex gag and goes out of his way to toss me away from Ramon. Then I query a bit and know the snake is my guy and he has something on his mind he would like to spill—or he wants Johnny to think so.

"In the morning I am not surprised to get a call from Ramon, who wants me to meet him at his hideaway office at one o'clock. We're going to talk and later go to a polo game. So I go—and I find him the same as I found the night watchman—beat up and cut up. So I grab Johnny and Morgie and they've got a neat alibi all set. It was Johnny who first let it sort of leak out that the redhead worked for Ramon as his secretary. He told us where she lived—was very co-operative, even knew exactly how much Ramon had taken from the joint the night before. He told me that Ramon was a shill, which was no surprise. It was also John's opinion that the girl had kayoed Ramon and pushed off with the dobies. So we go for that and trail Johnny to the airport and check him in on the Giant. The rest we've just had."

Terry said: "Then you think he and Morgie did kill Ramon?"

"We still don't know exactly what we think—but we don't eliminate your girl friend—she is in this somewhere up to her shell-pink ears, her fire-box locks, or what you have. You heard that accusation John made against you—about her tipping you off on how to win? That means they rigged that wheel you were playing. The dollerino was in on the works. She knew when it was time to win. Was she by any chance giving you the old tipperoo?"

"How could she, Dan? I didn't know her—"

"Well, maybe Johnny was imagining things. But a baby who is in on the rig in a gyp-joint is not usually a sweet thing. If she would do that, she might very easily have picked up that pound of sugar and dipsy-dewed—and that might be the handy little package she thought up for Ramon to give her—as John so kindly suggested."

Terry disagreed. "Her story still stands up—as she told it to me—and told me before we knew there was a murder."

"Before *you* knew there was a murder."

"No—I don't think she knew anything about it then. She was just explaining why she had suddenly picked up and left town."

"She had to tell you some kind of a story."

"No, she didn't."

"Then why did she?"

"Because I told her I couldn't understand how she had gotten herself mixed up with those people. Don't forget that she didn't have to mention that she was taking anything back—and if she had been in on any murder, she wouldn't have told me or anybody else that she had been with Ramon about the time he was knocked off—would she?"

"Did you ever hear of a prepared defense?"

"What good would it do her?"

"Well—she's got you arguing the weakest link in her defense right now as a strong link, hasn't she?"

"She wouldn't figure that fine."

"Listen, kid—when you figure murder, you can figure anything."

"I still believe her story—and I think Johnny has been trying to fasten it on her since the beginning."

Dan said to Tommy Donati: "Love is a wonderful thing, isn't it, Tommy?"

Terry ignored the jibe. "You still haven't explained the fact that Ramon was killed just after he had made a date to talk to you—and to keep him from talking to you—and that he was Johnny's alibi—and Johnny didn't want you to recognize him—how about that?"

Dan said to Tommy: "The kid's not a bad prospect, is he?"

"Very promising, I should say."

"All right," Dan said. "Let us dwell somewhat upon the matter suggested by the gentleman of the press—or the ex-gentleman of the press—remembering, of course, that we have now left the realm of fact and are now entering into the circles of speculation, the realm of super-sleuthing."

Dan stopped to light a cigarette. "If I had one of those fancy imported cigarettes I could do better on this. However, let's go back to the fateful night at the Golden Pheasant. Let's suppose Johnny and Morgie collaborated upon the neat little job there and that Raymond Torrance wandered in. Now John faces this problem: Should he buy off this blundering idiot or knock him off? In the old days there would have been one answer. Raymond would have been incased in cement for posterity. That, undoubtedly, was Morgie's suggestion.

"But Johnny has become a cutie with advancing years and he effects a compromise. If Raymond will provide the alibi that the watchman went bingo at the hands of a night marauder, Johnny will take him to Hollywood and make him a shill, give him a chance to be a big operator instead of a tin-horn. Raymond is not weighed down by morals—and let us say he has always wanted to see Hollywood. So it works out that way. So Raymond Torrance now becomes Ramon Toros. As a 'lucky' gambler and a first-class phony, he meets a lot of interesting people; he eases into the movies; women succumb to his charms, including some of John's dolls; he starts to do all right; he wants to break away from J. Duke; but J. Duke says no, my friend, you know too damn much and you also are a good shill—so you stay on the job.

"Now I drop in. Ramon sees a chance to use me. He plays up to me. The idea is to hold me as a club over J. Duke's head—he will break away or tell all, see? Now this was the way they left it Saturday night at the club. But after the ball is over, Cinderella Ramon is supposed to come back and shell in those G's which he won to fool the customers, and which are not stage money.

"But he doesn't show up the next morning. Chances are that J. Duke has been mistrusting Ramon for some time—he may even keep tab on his phone calls. Maybe he finds out about the call to me. So J. Duke and Morgie make a call on Ramon, via the usual fire escape. What do they find?"

Terry waited. "What do they?"

"That we don't know yet. Ramon may be dead or alive—if he is dead—Ruthie has done it. If he is alive, then Morgie and John take care of that slight detail. But that is speculation. The one thing we know is that the money is on the wing. J. Duke is not sap enough to go flying himself back into a murder rap for any doll—even one like this. Terry Moore is the kind of guy to do that little thing—or should I say Little Hercules? And, from the girl's own lips, we know she is carrying them there papers—so does she dress up so pretty now? Does she still come in as a pink silk angel?"

Terry was on his feet, excited. "Now let me speculate. We know Ramon was a gambler and he had a certain kind of guts. It looked to me like he wasn't afraid of Johnny Duke. Let's suppose what you say is true—that he wanted to get away from Johnny and go on his own. Suppose when you turned up he decided to play showdown. Then what happened at the Circle that night forced his hand a little. I pop off to Johnny and the girl, according to what she told me, realized she was in some kind of a spot and told Ramon she was through. He sees this as his chance. He advises her there is no time to lose—that she should get out of town on The Giant in the morning. He asks her to call at his office for a package. She gets it and leaves. Johnny and Morgie are on their way—maybe they see her, maybe they don't.

"But when they arrive, Ramon pushes his stack in. He bets Johnny that he will tell you about the Golden Pheasant if Johnny does not let him break away. Johnny threatens to kill him first. Then Ramon turns up his ace in the hole. He says that killing him would do no good because the story of what happened at the Golden Pheasant is already on its way back east with the money, which he considers his cut. He has the winning hand showing—but Johnny loses his head—as he did with me tonight—and kills him. After that there is nothing left for him to do but try to plant the crime on the girl—and then try to catch her and get the envelope she is carrying—with the money and the evidence? Now how does that stack up?"

Dan smiled, turned to Tommy Donati. "I think this new boy of ours would do much better on the writing end."

Tommy disagreed. "He's not bad, though."

Terry said: "Okay—have your fun—but I think there's as much reason for my diagnosis as yours. You've just made up your mind from the beginning that Ruth was no good."

"And you made up your mind that she was okay. Honest difference of opinion, that's all."

"You saw her and typed her right off. At least I've had a chance to talk to her."

"I'd love to meet her sometime, kid. See what you can do, huh? Tell her I've got a heart of gold, am good to my mother, love pets, but can't guarantee not to step on her feet in the rhumba."

"Suppose I did happen to run across her—would you give her a break—or not?"

"It's like I told you before, kid. In this business we have no friends—or enemies. We'll give her what's coming to her—no more, no less. What makes you think you might?"

"I have no rendezvous—if that's what you mean, but I believe she trusts me—"

"She certainly should."

"And she might just contact me—but I don't want you using me to catch her."

"Suspicious guy, isn't he, Tommy?" Dan turned to Terry. "You dig up the girl and tell her we'll give her a special rate—a discount for love or something like that. Instead of the hot seat, we might get it cut down to forty years."

Terry said: "The trouble with you, Dan, is that you never got off that burley que queen's lap."

Dan made owl eyes. "Maybe you've got something at that." He went to the window, locked it. "Keep that locked and your ears and eyes open. Don't talk to strangers in subways or you might get pushed off in front of a train. What I mean is—keep your left out. Things happened to J. Duke here tonight that will stew his brain. He might just blow his cupola—" Dan's hand came out of his pocket with a key. "Here, keep this. If you feel they're blowing lead breath at you again—go up to my place and live. Keep in touch with Tommy until I get back."

"Where are you going?"

"Back to the Coast—to check the rivets in Johnny's alibi. Keep punchin', Slugger."

After Dan and Tommy had gone, Terry stood looking at the key in his hand.

His apartment seemed very still.

CHAPTER XV

At the mirror, Terry stared very seriously into his own eyes, realized that he might now be dead. He looked about the apartment. If he were dead, cops, reporters, and photographers would be running all over the place. He knew every little thing they would do. Some guy, like himself, would come in and make a sketch. Carmichael would be around superintending everything. J. G. Carson would utter some grandiloquent phrases and cry some crocodile tears. There would be a funeral—oh, a helluva funeral; and the women would flock to see his body as they had to Valentino; then this other artist would draw Little Hercules and Terry Moore would be like Imperious Caesar, dead and turned to clay, stopping a hole to keep the wind away—or Alas, Poor Yorick, I knew him well—which amounted to the same thing.

He got to thinking about Ruth Allison in a different way, wondering if she were worth such a change in his existence; if she really did dress up as a pink silk angel with fire-box locks. Now that he looked back, there had been something unusual about that gambling scene; he had won every time she had smiled; Ramon had seemed to have been slightly amused at this—and Johnny had noted that Hercules, and not Ramon, was winning.

She *did* seem to know a lot about professional gambling—the house edge and such.

No, she didn't dress up quite so pretty now.

And Terry Moore didn't dress up so smart. If he were dead right now, they could put a one-word epitaph on his stone: DUMB. Before he went to bed Terry got down on his knees and uttered a fervent prayer to God, his Guardian Angel, and that special saint whose special duty it must be to look out for children, drunks, and people like Terry Moore.

Acting on a strong impulse he called Luella.

Her mother was sorry but Luella was not at home.

He slept lightly, was inordinately conscious of the city at night— its quarrels and hellos, its noises and inferences. He heard all the neighborhood sounds—cab drivers shouting at each other with harmless ferocity; occasional boat whistles from the river; the dim surf-like roar of traffic from trucks on First Avenue; and the periodic rattle of the elevated trains. All of these, on other nights, had formed the harmony of a New York lullaby; at least, Terry had not been conscious of them, being a young man of peaceful mind and healthful body.

But on other nights Terry Moore had had a job.

When daylight began to seep through the venetian blinds he relaxed and drifted off to delayed sleep as if the light was a wall that neither Johnny nor Morgie could vault.

Terry awoke at ten, animated by one decisive intention. He seemed to have snapped out of a nightmare, to be thinking clearly, to have returned to his proper mentality after a strange visit elsewhere. He definitely wanted out of this mess. He had been a fool to take up the battle for a girl, to have risked everything for her. He was lucky to be alive this morning, instead of talking it over somewhere with Ramon or Raymond or whatever had been his name.

He had difficulty shaving around his lip, where it was swollen. There was an abrasion on the bridge of his nose. His jaw felt sore. Of these marks and reminders Terry was a little proud, now that it was daylight. He wondered how the other fellow looked—the one swipe at Johnny's eye had been a good one. It still felt good.

It was eleven-thirty when he went to the lobby restaurant for breakfast. The papers were interesting—and warming. Terry never had thought he would see the day when he would be happy to see his own paper holding the bag; but, of course, it was not his own paper now—he had difficulty getting used to that idea.

Carmichael was on a hot spot. The headlines of all the afternoon papers screamed that the police were not interested in Johnny Duke, denied that they considered him involved in the Toros case; and ridiculed any idea of re-opening the Golden Pheasant murder. The police were still looking for Ruth Allison.

There was an interview with Johnny Duke that would rub salt in the Emperor's wounds. Johnny was inclined to be magnanimous about the *Leader* story. He said that he understood there were some newspapermen who thought more of circulation than accuracy. Johnny didn't mind. He could take it. Then he proceeded, rather cleverly, Terry thought, to capitalize the entire affair.

He explained his presence in New York as the longing of an old Broadwayite for native haunts. He wanted to make all of the old spots. He was on a holiday, he emphasized, and would rather not talk about unpleasant things like murder. He was now a business man of repute in Hollywood and would be well satisfied if people gave him a chance to go on being just that.

He very definitely had no ill-feeling toward Terry Moore. Johnny Duke was not quarreling with anybody about any girl—he was too old and too smart for that now. Ruth Allison had not been his girl, anyhow—she had been Ramon's girl. Johnny was not particularly interested in where she was. That was a job for the cops; and while J. Duke was definitely a law-and-order man now, he had not yet gone so far as to wear a badge.

About the mouse on his eye—well, he still went to the gym every day—and he had just forgotten to duck—that was all.

The late morning edition of the *Leader* was interesting. Terry knew there had been sweating in the city room. The gorgeous headlines of the early story involving Johnny Duke had been reduced to minor proportions. There was a clever job of straddling. The *Leader* was not giving up entirely on its story—but it also carried the statements of the police which knocked down the story. And there was, at the top of Kenny Tompkins' column, this unfraternal comment:

> The old gag about the red-headed girl being lucky has
> not worked out for Terry (Little Hercules) Moore.

Since his trail crossed that of Ruth Allison, he has been
in jail, has lost his sweetheart, and his job. And the
menace of a black hat is still in the background.

Another old newspaper pal, Terry thought—still sore because he
thought Terry had held out the Johnny Duke angle from the broadcast.

After breakfast, Terry went for a walk on Fifty-fourth Street,
west of Sixth Avenue. He covered the territory like a brush sales-
man, strolled slowly past every old brownstone house that had a sign
marked "Rooms For Rent." He could not knock on every door and ask
for Ruth Allison—he could only hope that she might see him from a
window. After awhile he knew he was being followed. He tested the
fellow by making stops for a cup of coffee, then for cigarettes. He
couldn't tell whether the fellow was a cop or one of Johnny Duke's
men. Then he suspected that another man was also in the game. He
crossed Eighth Avenue and went on to the Fifty-fourth Street police
station. He knew the place because he sometimes went there with
Dan to look in at night court.

He came out, took a cab, passed the two trailers on opposite sides
of the street. One of them went into the station. That was the cop.
The other followed in another cab. That would be Johnny Duke's man.

Cop business was tough business. Dan and Tommy hadn't actually made a promise not to tail him—but Terry felt let down, just the
same. He didn't know whether or not the girl was guilty—but he was
not going to lead the bird dogs to her door—the bird dogs from either
side of the law.

He decided to go to his office, pick up his stuff and get that over.
He would investigate the legal status of Hercules later—but win or
lose, he would never work again for Empire. He wanted nothing more
to do with J. G. Carson, Carmichael, or Tompkins. It wasn't going to be
easy to leave the people with whom he had worked for seven years—
but they probably wouldn't mourn over him. This was the newspaper
business.

When he entered the Empire Building at twelve o'clock he was
low and dismal, a man suddenly let down, a somewhat naive, trusting,

and friendly young man who had seen the contacts of years washed away in a few hours.

But human thought is an intangible, mercurial thing that is apt to change. In less than one hour Terry's world had been reconstructed, was stronger than ever before.

The men around the office had come to sympathize—to cuss old Carmichael as a striped-hipped hyena, Kenny Tompkins as a complete louse doubled in civet; and J. G. Carson as sufficient reason for the abolition of the capitalistic system. Their voices were low, because of J. G.'s suspected ogpu, but their voices were comforting.

Then Kenny Tompkins dropped in and made a sort of apology, said he had Terry to thank for Carmichael drying on that limb, instead of himself, and that he would make it right in the next day's column.

There came a summons from J. G. Carson.

Terry went to the floor above with blood in his eye and his voice and his heart. It was time somebody told the old Emperor where to take off and Terry was in the mood.

But Terry did little talking. He didn't get a chance. The Emperor talked vaguely out the window; it was difficult to guess his intended course from the tenor of his opening remarks. He took a second look at Terry and cried: "Who cut your face up that way?"

"I went to a gym."

"Did Johnny Duke dare to lay his hands on you?"

"He went to a gym, too."

"Did you give him that eye?"

Terry grinned. "I suppose."

"Well, I'll be switched. Hercules—I'm proud of you. I'm proud that we have a man in our organization who has the courage to defend a defenseless woman—and the courage to stand on his own feet against a ruthless killer." The Emperor was off on one of his flights of bombast—but Terry cut him short.

"That's all very nice, Mr. Carson—but I'm not in your organization—and your organization has stolen Little Hercules with one of Carmichael's trick contracts—"

"What's all this?" The Emperor rang for his secretary.

Twenty minutes later Terry was back in his cubbyhole, the fair-haired boy of Empire, without a doubt. He had a new contract, a stout raise, and he was responsible hereafter only to the Emperor, who was going to make Little Hercules the biggest thing in the history of features—a new idea, the projection of a forceful personality through a comic strip.

And Little Hercules belonged irrevocably to Terry Moore.

As Terry unpacked, he felt very kindly toward Johnny Duke and the opportunity to hang a mouse on his eye.

He even felt kindly toward Carmichael.

He heard the shuffle of the one o'clock sight-seeing group coming along goldfish corridor. Terry turned his back—but he could not close his ears to the stereotyped speech. He knew it by heart:

"And in this office, ladies and gentlemen, you see Terry Moore, the famous creator of Little Hercules, actually at work depicting the further adventures of the funny little man who daily delights the fifty million readers of 387 newspapers, undoubtedly the greatest success in all newspaper history. Mr. Moore is at the moment, as you see, concentrating so intensely on his work that he is unaware of our presence here. And, of coarse, we do not wish to disturb the mood of a great artist."

Everybody around the shop seemed to know the speech. Every so often a pilgrim on his way from one great journalistic moment to another, would stop and deliver it verbatim, and finish with applause. At such comrades Terry sometimes made derisive gestures with his fingers; but he now had to forego even this resistance because he forgot once, and did it while the sightseers were looking, which embarrassed him completely, for the crowd was made up mostly of women.

Now he religiously kept his back turned and gave no indication that he knew the hourly group was standing at his window, that the guide had made his stereotyped speech. Which explained why he was completely unaware, until she stood before him, that Ruth Allison had been in the group.

CHAPTER XVI

Terry was shocked into momentary speechlessness by the sharp change in her. She was nervous; her face was much thinner; her eyes were distressed.

"Ruth," he said slowly, "you shouldn't have come here."

"I had to see you—talk to you."

Carmichael was coming down the hall. Terry said: "Give me something from your purse—quick—you've come in here for an autograph."

She fumbled with her purse, could find nothing, looked inept. He frowned, reached into his file, came up with a used strip, wrote on it: "Lounge, Music Hall, today, three o'clock." Handed it to her. "Beat it—pretend you've gotten away with something. Hurry." He turned his back.

She left, a plain girl in glasses and a thin coat, too light for the chill air—but apparently a happy girl, a girl who had crashed a gate and now had in her possession an autographed Hercules strip. Terry followed to the corridor, saw that she had rolled the strip into a thin tube and put it in her purse by the time she had caught up with the rest of the sightseers.

As Carmichael passed, Terry grumbled: "If somebody doesn't tell those guides to keep their damned sightseers out of my office, I'll see that it's done." He banged his door, grinned as he heard a loud grunt, which was Carmichael's acknowledgment that his pampered Hollywood big shot had threatened to go to J. G.

He was going to have fun with Carmichael.

Terry sat looking at his board. Ruth's appearance had numbed him. The girl had been through things. She had missed sleep, perhaps she had missed food. She was on edge and getting ready to crack. She had something better than a disguise to shield her now. It would be hard to see in this girl any resemblance to the glamorous American Beauty which the public, and the police, had been led to believe was Ruth Allison.

At two-thirty Terry left the building by the freight elevator, walked to the corner and took a cab to Radio City. He went to the corner drug store, had a sandwich and a malted milk, ambled into the theater and sauntered down to the lounge. People were coming and going. This place had come to mind, he supposed, because he had always thought it would be a perfect spot for clandestine meetings. He had seen people he suspected of being secret lovers get together there, although more likely they were legally, if not always happily married.

Terry had never pictured himself coming here to a secret meeting; up to now there had been no secrets about his life. But, he admitted as he slowly went down the heavily carpeted steps, even had he imagined himself in such a meeting, he would not have made it as daring as this one would seem—meeting a girl wanted by police and gangsters. In fiction, or on the screen upstairs, this would be built up into terrific tenseness; but here he was just walking down the steps, lighting a cigarette, as if he were just another person in New York with nothing more important to do that afternoon than go to the movies.

There were not many people in the lounge. Terry saw immediately that if he met Ruth here they would be conspicuous. Too many people knew his face by now—and any girl seen with him was under suspicion.

He waited until ten minutes after three, then went into the men's room, brushed up and came out. Ruth was coming from the powder room. Their paths would cross near the big bronze statue. Luella had once paused here to give him the story significance of the statue. Now Terry paused, as if he were an art student. Ruth was near him. He said, to the statue: "Upstairs."

This was all so simple and unexciting, so little like fiction or a play. He went upstairs, inside the lower floor, saw that Ruth was following. There were patches of empty seats. Terry took one of these. In a little while she came to the seat beside him. It was dark and they could talk without attracting attention or being overheard. Other couples were off to themselves in the same manner.

She removed her glasses. Their eyes had not yet become accustomed to the darkness but he could see that his first impression had been correct. "Ruth—you don't look well."

"I know."

"You shouldn't have come to the office."

"I had to see you."

"But Kenny Tompkins suspects you have black hair."

"Oh—how?"

"He remembered you from a Broadway show."

"I didn't think I was on long enough in that for anybody to remember me. Terry—I'm so sorry for all the trouble I've caused you."

"What trouble?"

"I read in Tompkins' column—"

"Oh, that. Say, he did me a favor. I've got a new contract and everything's better than ever."

"I'm so glad. Was it true about—Luella?"

"She's a little upset—but she'll get over it."

"How about Johnny?"

He couldn't resist boasting: "Johnny and I have become old buddies since I saw you last. We meet quite often. He was at my place—only last night—"

"Oh, Terry, no. Was that what—bruised your face?"

"I suppose."

"And did you—did you give Johnny the mouse?"

"Nobody else." He was proud as a seven-year-old.

"Oh, Terry, that's marvelous." She was laughing softly as though deeply amused at the idea.

"Then," he said, "and somewhat fortunately, Dan came in."

"And what happened?"

"I don't think Johnny will come calling on me again."

"That's fine." They could see better now. She smiled a little sadly. "Well, then, you're all right."

"I'm great—never better."

"I'm glad to know that, anyhow."

"You shouldn't have come, Ruth."

"But what else could I do if I caused you all that trouble? Anyhow, I wanted to."

"Any girl seen talking to me is under suspicion. Why didn't you call?"

"I thought they might be tracing your calls. And I thought it would be safe enough to go through with the other people. And you would have lied to me—I wanted to see for myself. Maybe you're lying to me now about your job—and Johnny."

"No—it's the truth, thanks be."

"Then you're all right—and thanks for the tip about Tompkins!" Their eyes met. Hers were obviously saying that this was the end of the story. She gave his hand a final, affectionate pat, whispered, "I'll never forget you," and started to rise.

"Wait, Ruth—"

"But it's dangerous for you, Terry."

He caught her hand. "But I want to talk to you first."

Her fingers were small and warm—and nervous. They were clutching at him as if he were salvation. His hand closed firmly over hers. "You poor kid," he said. "You poor kid."

He knew she was crying. She was quiet but her body was relaxed and inclined toward him. Terry said nothing, gave his eyes to the picture.

His reason couldn't wipe out the logic of Dan's evidence against her; but Terry knew one thing—this girl had done no murder. This girl wasn't bad. His heart told him that—and told him that she needed help if any of God's creatures ever did.

To any prying eyes, they must have looked like lovers. She roused when the program changed, and a new musical rhythm flamed through the theater. She awoke with a start; then, when her eyes saw him, the look in them touched him.

"Look, Ruth," he said seriously, "you can't go on like this, ducking and hiding always."

"I know."

"Ruth—have you delivered that package Ramon gave you?"

"Not yet. When I get that off my mind, I'm going away."

"That won't be easy. Dan is sure that Ramon was Raymond Tor-rance; he may have Ramon's friends—or relatives—under observa-tion."

"I'll have to take that chance."

"But if you do deliver it, and get away, you'll still be a fugitive. I can see what it's doing to you."

"But what can I do?"

"Let me open that package."

She looked at him, with gradually narrowing eyes. "I promised to deliver it."

"But it may have the information to clear you."

"I couldn't break my promise to a dead man."

"He wouldn't want you to go through what you're going through—particularly if that letter would convict Johnny Duke of his murder."

"What makes you think it would?"

"I'm not sure—but I've got a pretty good idea."

"I can't let you do anything more. Please let me go now, Terry, and you'll be out of it. Please."

He restrained her. "Ruth—look at me." She faced his eyes. "Are you sure Ramon gave you that letter to deliver?"

"Terry!"

"I've got to know."

"I've asked you just to let me go and forget me."

"I can't forget you, Ruth. And I've talked to Dan about you—"

She gasped. "Oh, no—"

"But why not? I told him I thought you were not mixed up in this seriously; he said that if I could prove that, he would help you. This letter may be just what all of us want. Dan told me, if I saw you, to see what was in this letter."

"You told him about it?"

"I thought it was the wise thing to do."

"But he'll think—"

When she hesitated, he finished the sentence: "That it contains money—and you stole it? Yes, he thinks that. I told him that it might contain the money, but that you didn't steal it."

"Why does he think I would steal it?"

"Ruth—did you know Ramon worked for Johnny?"

"Was that it?"

"Johnny said that Ramon was a shill and you were a part of the setup—and knew what was going on!"

Her voice came slowly, softly: "Do you believe that, Terry?"

"No. I told them so." But he proceeded, stubbornly. "Then Johnny said you had tipped me off how to beat his game that night." When she did not answer, he continued, resolutely: "I was playing whenever you smiled."

"Did you think, then, I was tipping you?"

"No—I just thought you were lucky."

"Well, I was tipping you."

"Ruth—"

"But it wasn't just cheating. I kept figures for Ramon on how he played. I thought he studied them and got his system from that. After awhile, I began to get the system, or thought I did. At least, certain things seemed to happen in a series. I wasn't always right but it worked out pretty much that way."

"But why did you want to see me win?"

"It wasn't so much that I wanted to see you win as that I didn't want to see you lose. I had begun to get an idea that the game was rigged. You looked like the type who might risk much more than you could afford—which you certainly are. But if Ramon was a shill—and I can easily believe that now—I wasn't supposed to know it, Terry—and I didn't. I suppose I was just there as part of the script—as background for Ramon's front."

"What else did you do at the office—besides furnish these figures?"

"Oh, I compiled charts on all sorts of things—racing, football, politics—Ramon was a scientific gambler. I made bets for him at times. It was so unsavory that all I needed was that final push—which seems to have come too late."

"Did Johnny know about this office?"

"He came there often—usually in the morning; sometimes they quarreled, frequently toward the end."

"Ruth—look at me again—and tell me I haven't been wrong on you—with your own lips."

She looked at him steadily until her eyes welled with tears. "I swear it, Terry, by my dead mother."

He swallowed, pressed her fingers. "We're getting out of here."

"But we can't be seen together."

"I'll take you home then, and we can talk in the cab. Where are you living?"

"I'm on Thirty-ninth Street now. I had to change this noon."

Terry spoke quickly: "What street were you on?"

"I went back to Fifty-fourth—but to-day I was afraid somebody was looking for me."

Terry swore. "I've been making it tough on you. I walked along Fifty-fourth Street this morning, hoping you would see me—until I knew I was being tailed. Sure they haven't seen you?"

"I wouldn't think so."

"No wonder you look like you do. Ruth, we've got to stop all this. We've got to find a place where you'll be safe until we can dope out what to do. I've got a hunch you never should go back to where you've been stopping—is there any reason why you have to?"

"I've been a country girl with a canvas suitcase. If I just disappear, they may get suspicious and get my description."

"That's right. Well, we'll go back there and pick up your suitcase and then we'll go somewhere and take a look at that letter."

"I don't know, Terry—"

"The address might tell us something—and then I could deliver it myself and maybe put Dan on the trail of the person. See anything wrong in that?"

"Except that I still don't think you should involve yourself again—"

"A little more won't hurt. Anyhow. I'm working with the cops now—"

"Can you trust them? I mean, Terry, I'm willing to put myself in your hands—but can you be so sure about them doing what they promise?"

"They're as safe as the Supreme Court." Terry wasn't so sure as he pretended. After all, he had been tailed by two men—one, he was sure, was a cop. But that was a minor item now. The urgent thing was to get Ruth in a place where they could talk, where she wouldn't have to run like a thief, where she could get a night's sleep, where she could be free from Johnny Duke—where they could look at that letter.

Terry grinned. He would put her on the east side of town—then he would take a walk on a new street on the west side every day and keep those bird dogs busy. He would locate the person to whom Ramon was sending the money and envelope, tip Dan off, and then it wouldn't matter so much about Ruth. He said to her: "Now put on those cheaters and follow me at a safe distance, as though you were a woman from the old country."

"Simpleton."

Terry thought it would probably be a lot of fun to bum around with Ruth when she got out from under the rap.

They made a taxicab, apparently free from observation. It was a short drive to the address she gave, on a street of once proud homes which were now old boarding houses, the type of street in the business section where people park their cars for hours. It was filled with such cars, mostly jammed together, and all empty except a medium-priced sedan where a man sat back of the wheel, with a newspaper in his hand.

Terry looked at the man, said to the driver: "Never mind stopping, just take us around the corner to the nearest subway. Step on it—I've forgotten something."

Ruth was looking at Terry with wide eyes. The car picked up speed. Terry turned, saw the driver wrestling the sedan out of the traffic line.

There was a subway kiosk just around the corner. "Right here," Terry called. They entered the subway, waited inside the door. The taxicab picked up another fare and drove away as the black sedan rumbled around the corner and sped down the street.

"Ruth—have you got that envelope with you?"

She nodded. He took her arm and they went into the subway. "I think that was Johnny's man. And he knows we're together. You can't go back for your clothes—the cop might be there."

They were in the Times Square station. The shuttle train was waiting to go. Terry was thinking, talking. "You're not safe on the streets any longer—thanks to my blundering. You're not safe with me—"

The bell of the shuttle train was clanging. Terry was jingling keys in his pocket. Without warning he dragged Ruth with him, caught the sliding train door. It opened again, automatically closed after them as they pushed in against the rest of the human sardines.

She was breathless. "What is it?"

"Merely thought reaction." He pressed her arm, looked deep into her eyes through the cheap spectacles. "You can begin to relax, child— I've got just the apartment you need."

"Not your place, Terry,—I won't let you do that."

"Not my place—Dan's place."

CHAPTER XVII

They were sitting in one of the side-pocket restaurants in the cavity of Grand Central. Terry's humor was light from the froth of his jest. "Better eat a hearty meal—you may not get another for awhile—unless you can cook."

Her eyes were bright, her face flushed, her voice uncertain. "But, Terry—I'm afraid."

"It's a perfect setup. He's gone to the Coast again—he gave me the key—to hide from Johnny Duke."

"And you're hiding me—won't he be angry?"

"He won't know you're there until I tell him. All we want is time to decide what to do." A new thought disturbed him. "Ruth, you trust me, don't you?"

"When I can't trust you—"

"It'll be all right—once I get you in. And that should be easy after what you've been through." He took a paper napkin and began to draw diagrams with a pencil.

It was early dark and the evening rush hour was beginning when they joined the cross-currents of humanity that shuffled across 42nd and Lexington like molecules under a microscope.

Terry took a cab and Ruth started walking. He wanted to get there first; and he thought she would attract less attention if she came on foot; instead of arriving at the house by car.

His cab drove to the middle entrance. Terry looked about carelessly as he paid the fare. He went to the newsstand and inspected the lobby. Satisfied that there were no bird dogs about, he strolled through the connecting corridor to his own lobby and went to the desk.

There were no messages.

He opened the door to his own apartment, snapped on the light before entering. The living-room was empty. He left the door slightly ajar, carefully searched the bedroom, discarded his coat and hat, opened the window to the fire escape, looked up and down the building wall.

He left the lights burning in his apartment, took the stairway to the roof, hurried along a familiar path between the penthouse and his side of the building, and entered another door. He was in a narrow corridor where garbage cans and floor mops were stored. This led to a boxlike foyer about five feet square, from which opened the doors to the elevator and the three penthouses on the middle roof.

He entered one of these apartments and closed the door. "Dan?" he called. When there was no answer, he went quickly through the place, came back to the door, opened it slightly and waited.

This was the dangerous moment before the armistice.

The elevator was coming. Terry's quaking thoughts began to kick at his solar plexus. This was something he hadn't thought of. Ruth was due any moment—suppose she arrived as the elevator opened to discharge a tenant for one of the other apartments? Any stranger would be questioned.

The elevator came to the top floor. There was talk. Then the elevator descended, and somebody went into the apartment at the front of the house. When the door to the garbage corridor began to open slowly, Terry gave a soft signal. Ruth ran lightly across the corridor and was safely inside, breathing deeply.

Her eyes made Terry Moore feel humble and unworthy of what he saw. Impulsively her arms went about his neck and she buried her head on his shoulder.

Finally she looked up, pulled shyly away from his arms, as if he were a doctor whose professional services were no longer needed. She took a cigarette from her bag, and went to the one big chair in the room. Terry pulled the shades, then turned on the lights. "Wouldn't want to start gossip on an old bachelor like Dan. What happened?"

"The lobby was crowded and so was the elevator. When it began to thin out, I got off on the sixteenth floor and came the rest of the way by the stairs. I was in the corridor outside when the elevator stopped here. If anybody had found me there I believe I would have screamed. I guess I'm just about at the end of my rope."

"No—you'd have come up with a mop and become a maid."

She smiled. "I already had a mop in my hand."

"You can use a drink. Dan is always the perfect host." He went to the kitchen, returned with one drink, gave it to her. "Here's luck, milady."

"Thank you. How about you?"

"No—sometimes it makes me do funny things. I'll be night watchman. You start to relax."

She leaned back in the comfortable chair. "After the last week, this is heaven."

He said, almost to himself: "Heaven."

"What did you say?"

"I was just thinking about a story of two men and their grandmothers—and heaven. It's a story about viewpoint—and background, I suppose. Tell you about it sometime."

Ruth was the type of girl who didn't insist that a man tell her what he was thinking. Or perhaps she was just too tired. She closed her eyes. Terry busied himself about the kitchen and bedroom. When he returned, Ruth opened her eyes. "I seem to have had a few minutes' nap."

"Don't let me stop you—go right ahead."

"No—that will do me for awhile. My mind seems like a radio—every time somebody turns a button it starts going—and is full of noise and static." She stood, flexed, smiled enigmatically. "I hope Cousin Dan doesn't mind too much my dropping in this way—I certainly am enjoying it."

"Oh, he'd only be sorry he doesn't know about it. I'm sure he'd hustle right back."

"Not that kind of jokes, Terry, please." But her face and voice seemed refreshed. "Well, I suppose I might as well look over the old homestead—and sort of get organized."

Dan's place was called a three-room penthouse, which was technically true, because there were dividing walls; actually the entire layout was about the size of a big living-room. The "kitchen" was a masterpiece of compactness, with a gas stove, sink and refrigerator—and space to turn around. The living room was a small square, with table, studio couch, a large cabinet radio and a few chairs. French doors opened on a terrace that looked over the East River.

Terry stopped at the doors. "I imagine the terrace should be out of bounds this evening—but when the winds are right, you get a delicious waft from the packing plants." He checked the lock. "That," he said, as they passed the bathroom, "is the bathroom—which will be all right, if you like a shower—"

"I do—"

"That's fine. And this is the bedroom, which is a good name for it because it is about big enough, as you can see, to hold a bed and a chest of drawers. Sorry we have no make-up table or mirror—Dan didn't know you were coming!' He went to the windows which looked out on the terrace. "Suggest you keep these locked and get your air from the bathroom window—it's not wide enough for anybody to crawl through."

They went back to the living-room. Ruth said: "Dan lives very comfortably for a bachelor, doesn't he?"

"He likes to live well. Of course, he does a certain amount of entertaining."

"I see." She looked at the studio couch. "Do you live well, too?"

"I have a little more room space—you see, I don't have a terrace. It doesn't sound quite so good as a penthouse, but it's more comfortable. You must drop down and see me sometime—just across the roof and down one flight."

"I'll try to do that." She looked over the place again. "Well, I suppose you gentlemen of Broadway must lead interesting lives."

"You wouldn't be a nosey kind of guest, would you, young lady? I mean, go around hunting for letters and things like that?"

"I'll try to restrain my curiosity up here, anyhow; but I warn you to watch me when I come down to your place."

"You wouldn't find anything. Both Dan and I are monastic. In the absence of the owner, I've been sort of looking around. I hooked up the refrigerator. There are enough towels and linen to last a week or so, I imagine—if you're sparing. Now—how about that cooking?"

"What do you like?"

"Do you mean—I'm invited for dinner sometime?"

"Any time."

"Okay, tomorrow night then. I'll smuggle in some stuff in the morning for your breakfast—" He grinned. "Now, I've been checking and find we have no ladies' department—second floor, lingerie, pajamas, so-and-so's and such-and-such—which should prove to you what kind of a guy Dan is—but if you want a toothbrush or anything like that, just give me a list and I'll get those, too."

"I'll manage."

"Play the radio low, so the neighbors don't get tough. These walls are regular sounding boards. And I wouldn't keep it on after ten-thirty."

"I'll be asleep the minute you leave."

"Is that a hint?"

"You know it isn't." She looked at her watch. "It's only seven-twenty-five."

He made himself comfortable on the studio couch. "Then I can stay awhile. I had a girl once whose dad made me go home at ten o'clock."

"How old were you?"

"Sixteen."

"I'll bet you've had many a girl."

"I know you've done all right."

They talked about his old girls and her old boy friends—all of whom were, of course, quite young. They talked easily. There were few lulls. In one of these, Terry looked at her searchingly and asked: "Have I known you only a week?"

"Five days, really—but very long days." She shook her head. "How very long."

He got up and started walking around. "Well—I have an idea that will soon be over."

An unexplained quiet came over them. Terry became ill at ease, turned on the radio. There was dance music. The girl seemed to be napping again. The program changed and she awoke. "Sorry," she said, "I'm like a sleepy old cat."

Kenny Tompkins was on the air. He rattled off the war bulletins and Washington news. Then:

"Terry (Little Hercules) Moore, exclusively reported in my column this morning as having lost his job as a result of the Johnny Duke story, is back on the payroll with a new contract and sitting pretty. Terry was not responsible for the Johnny Duke story. However, Little Hercules came to work today with a cut lip and other facial abrasions—and Johnny Duke is around town with a mouse over his eye. The story now circulated is that they went to the same gym—and that Little Hercules can take care of himself in the flesh as well as in the comic strip. Shake hands, boys—and forget it. Meanwhile Dan Colby came in from the Coast and has left again via the skyways.

"Police are still searching for Ruth Allison. They will have a better chance of finding her if they look for a girl with black hair—the red hair was a transformation. They probably will find her in a theatrical boarding house. Ruth—where are you?"

Terry chuckled: "And wouldn't you be surprised? And you're a little late with that scooper."

Ruth was looking at Terry with solemn eyes. "I'd be shaking apart right now—if I were still alone." She opened her bag, withdrew a long envelope of very stiff paper, looked at it for a moment, handed it to Terry. "There it is, just as he gave it to me. I don't know what it might say. Before you open it, I want to tell you again that everything I've said to you has been true."

Terry slowly ripped open the envelope, withdrew five hundred dollars in bills, another, small envelope, sealed and addressed, and a folded sheet. "This is for you," he said.

"I would rather you read it."

CHAPTER XVIII

Terry read:

> Miss Allison:
> Many things may have happened by the time you reach New York. This may even be a voice from the dead, pleading that the enclosed letter be delivered to my wife. It contains money.
>
> I have called Dan Colby and am to see him at noon. If anything happens to prevent that, please tell Mr. Colby that what he suspects is true, regarding the Golden Pheasant—that if anything happens to me, it will be by the hands of the same two men—because I knew too much to allow me to break away from them, as I wish.
>
> I am sorry to have involved you in my unhappy affairs and I hope this errand will take you safely out of danger. If you need a friend I think that young cartoonist is a man you could depend upon.
>
> I am enclosing money which you may need to locate my wife. Please protect her identity—that is the one decent thing I have done for her.
>
> R. T.

The sealed envelope was addressed to Mrs. Ray Torenzo in a small town on Long Island. Terry said: "Johnny and Morgie killed him. This is proof enough." He looked at the other envelope he had in his hand. "If we only knew what he says in here."

"We can't open it, Terry. Not after what he's written. I've got to deliver that to his wife."

"We can have the police locate her—"

"But there's money in that envelope. If the police get it you can't tell how they'll tie it up—and he asked me to protect her, to keep her out of it. She may know too much, too."

She had wilted again. Terry noticed it. "How about another drink?"

"Before I go to bed."

She was fighting to control her nerves. Her lips were quivering, her teeth chattering. He sat on the arm of the chair, held her trembling hand. She said: "I'll be all right in a moment. It's the reaction, I suppose."

"Sure. You know what this means, Ruth?"

"I'm not so sure."

"Well, it means you'll be all right—and I'm not such a sap as a lot of people have thought. Now look, I think you ought to go to bed now and get a good night's sleep."

"I haven't slept for a week, really."

"Well, I'll mix you a hot toddy that will have you pounding your ear like a runaway engine. Then tomorrow we'll locate his wife and see what's in that envelope. If it says the right things—or if his wife does—we'll send for Dan. He'll pin Johnny's ears back—and then we'll all live happily ever after."

"Just like that, eh?"

"Any objections?"

She did not answer. Terry went to the kitchen and lit the gas stove. Her eyes were closed. She wore a simple dress of cheap, blue cloth. Her hair was in purposeful disarray. Her stockings were cotton and her shoes sturdy. All of this Terry noted as he waited for the water to boil. She had done a good job of make-up. And she must have done a good job of acting.

"Know what I was just thinking?" he called from the kitchen. "I was thinking that Hollywood couldn't see you as an actress in one of their flimflam dramas—and yet, you've been starring in a drama that has entertained the country."

"Ably supported by Terry Moore." She went to the mirror in the bathroom, did a few tricks and came out a different girl. Her face seemed fresh and young again, and there was sparkle in her eyes.

He was stirring the toddy. "I'll be in for breakfast—hope you don't starve until I get here."

She stretched toward the ceiling: "Sleep!" Her eyes were telling him thanks. Impulsively he said: "You've got a lot of guts, kid."

"Terry—did you tell Luella you kissed me?"

"I'm not a guy who kisses and tells." He wrote his phone number on Dan's desk pad. "If anything should come up, call me. I'll be here in a few minutes. Otherwise, it would be just as well if the operator doesn't know."

She followed to the door. Her eyes were large and uncertain. "Terry—"

"Yes?"

"Would you think it awful if I asked you to stay here tonight?"

"Certainly not."

"There are two rooms. I believe I could really sleep then."

"Sure. I'll tell you what. I'll go down and get some stuff for breakfast and the morning papers. Then I'll be back—about a half hour."

"I'll say good night now, Terry."

He said: "Good night, Ruth."

"Good night, Little Hercules." She kissed him lightly.

When Terry returned the door to the bedroom was closed. He sat down with the early morning papers. There were no new developments on the case. The Golden Pheasant angle had been abandoned and Johnny Duke was apparently in the clear. So, it was beginning to be accepted, was Ruth Allison. Terry's practiced eye sensed that the story was beginning to fade. He smiled, realized that he was in the process of building up a sensation which would excite every city room in the town.

He played the radio softly and finally went to bed at 11 o'clock, which was a new record for him. He lay long in the dark, eyes open, faintly conscious of the rumble of the trucks, the roar of the trains, the blasts from river boats. His eyes were on the door to the bedroom and his mind was on the girl who he assumed would be getting a well-merited sleep.

This situation was the most bizarre of all he had encountered in the brief five days of the revolution Ruth Allison had brought to his life. The police of the country were looking for this girl. Dan Colby was on the Coast—and the girl for whom he was searching was in

Dan's bed. Terry grinned in the dark. He was looking forward to the time when Dan would find out.

He thought of Luella and her reactions, doubted if her sense of propriety would ever withstand this shock. Terry admitted that it would look very bad if people found out; but it was all simple and normal enough. All of his relations with Ruth Allison had been similar—very normal and quite pleasant in themselves but highly dramatic to other people. He admitted that he liked the prescription; thought that it might be a very interesting program of living. Certainly, at least up to now, he had never had a dull moment with Ruth; yet the moments had all been very simple and logical.

But, Terry admitted, while all this was very exciting, it would not do for a steady diet. One just couldn't live in such tension and live very long. One might not live very long as it was—as witness the events of last night when Terry had felt that he was about to pass forever from this earth. Nor did he know what might come out of this new adventure. He was about to provide evidence which would convict two of the most dangerous criminals in America of murder. It was all right for the police to do that because it was their job and their victims seemed to hold no intense resentment against them; but Terry was not a cop. Well, he was in so deep now that the only thing left was to go through with it; he was satisfied that Ruth Allison was the victim of circumstances and he could not let her down. But when this was over, he would say good-by to the girl of excitement and go back with hat in hand to Luella, and to everything that she represented, which was Terry's normal pace.

He picked up the desk phone which was near the studio couch, made a call in a very low voice.

"Luella?"

"Yes?"

"This is Terry."

"Yes?"

"I just thought I'd call and see how you were."

There was a slight hesitation. Then her voice, a strange, unfamiliar voice which he had never suspected could come out of Luella, said: "You have humiliated me so completely that I cannot face my friends. That item in Tompkins' column this morning was just too much."

"But Luella, this will all be over very soon and I promise you—"

"You needn't bother. I will not share you with a public character."

"But, Luella, you don't realize what you're saying—"

"I realize perfectly. Let me state it another way. Until you get that woman out of your life, please don't ever call me again."

Terry lay staring at the closed door. He wondered why he didn't feel much more badly about this, decided that it probably had something to do with the fact that Ruth was sleeping in the next room and that Luella was in far-away Brooklyn. Anyhow, there was nothing he could do about it at the moment.

Once, after twelve, the elevator came all the way to the top floor and stopped. Terry was wide awake but it proved to be only a tenant of one of the other apartments.

Terry thought of Johnny Duke and Morgie. This would be very simple for them. Terry and the girl would be found dead. Their reputations would be forever blackened. The Ramon Toros murder case would be closed. Dan Colby might be ruined as a detective.

Yes, Johnny and Morgie could do all right with this situation.

It was daylight before Terry slept—yet he slept so surprisingly well that he did not know, in the morning, that anybody was in the room until he became aware that Dan Colby was shaking him, saying: "Wake up, kid—what happened? Did they make a pass at you?"

"What are you doing back here, Dan?"

"I flew right back."

Terry was staring at the bedroom door, where Ruth Allison was standing, wearing one of Dan's pajama coats as a makeshift robe which came below her knees. Dan's eyes went to the bedroom door just before it closed again. He turned to Terry Moore, scowling, "Well, I'll be a dirty—"

Terry yawned a grin. "Take it easy, Dan."

"After all—I gave you my key to protect you, not for you to make a love nest out of my place."

Terry was sitting up. "The trouble with you, Dan, as I have said before, is that you never got off that burley que queen's lap."

Dan's eyes melted and then a slow grin broke over his face. "You wouldn't mean to tell me that this is—"

Terry smiled. "You guessed it. Now listen. Everything's kosher. I located her last night. Johnny's guys were waiting at her house so I had to bring her here. She was afraid to stay alone. I was going to get in touch with you—"

"Yeh? Why didn't you tell Tommy?"

"I wanted the kid to get one night's sleep before you coppers started barking at her. Now, if you'll behave like a gentleman, we'll invite you to breakfast."

Dan, still talking to himself, went to the radio and slipped down a button attachment on the side. A voice answered: "Yeh?"

Dan said: "Tommy—"

"Got in, did you?"

"And what I found! Can you come over right away?"

"Soon as I get breakfast."

"Oh, come right over—we're having breakfast here—guests of Little Hercules—and friend."

CHAPTER XIX

Dan switched the button.

Terry asked: "What's that gadget?"

"Something you missed—a two-way radio that connects Tommy's place and mine—and our cars and Headquarters." He shook his head slowly. "Well, I thought I'd been around and seen things—but this is a new one for the book."

"You told me to bring in the girl, didn't you? Then what are you squawking about?"

A slow grin spread over Dan's face. "Have I been squawking?"

"I don't know what else you would call it?"

"Then I'm sorry." He sat down. "I'm just not used to the idea yet. I give a pal my key to hide out from the menace while I go to the Coast to look for a doll—and as soon as I get over Newark my pal brings the doll I'm looking for into my place. Sonny boy, that's as neat a little cross as I ever heard of."

"How about the guy who told me I wouldn't be tailed if I looked for the girl—and who has me tailed from that time on?"

"That was just to keep an eye on you—for your safety."

"Oh, I see. And if your man happened to run into the girl at the same time, he couldn't help that, could he?"

"While we're on the general subject, Terry, how long have you been holding out on me about this black hair gag?"

"Since the train."

"I see—you knew it when you gave us that picture?" Dan shook his head sadly. "Well, Boy Scout, you beat me again—by a day."

"You knew it that long?"

"In going through Ramon's accounts we found a bill. The chiseler hadn't paid for the job—imagine that. So we did a little checking and found it had been made for Ruthie—so we let her think we didn't—"

The bedroom door opened.

Terry said: "You two know each other, I believe?"

Dan bowed elaborately. "Glad to see you again, Miss Allison—very glad. Welcome to our little home. Sorry I wasn't here to greet you—but I trust my boy here took care of everything."

"He was very sweet."

"I don't doubt it."

Ruth was uncertain. Terry said lightly: "Oh, Ruth, we're having two guests for breakfast. Fortunately I laid in enough supplies. Do you mind?"

"Not at all." Her lip was curving pleasantly.

Terry started for the bathroom. "Come on, Dan, I want to talk to you."

Dan said, "No, I think I'll watch Miss Allison cook the eggs. I'm very particular about my eggs."

Terry called to Ruth: "Until I get back, Ruth—just talk about eggs." When the bathroom door had closed, Dan said: "That Hercules is a wonder."

"He's a darling."

"From your standpoint, he should be."

"From my standpoint he is." Ruth walked to the kitchen. She was fresh, captivating, even in the formless cotton dress. Dan followed. His big frame filled the door space. "Mind if I make myself comfortable?"

"Please do." She was opening the packages Terry had brought. Dan removed his coat, pulled up a chair, teetered on its two back legs. She asked: "How do you like your eggs, Mr. Colby? Hard-boiled?"

"That's the way I usually get them but I like them scrambled."

"With plenty of ketchup, I suppose?"

"How did you know?"

"I guessed. Where do you keep your sugar?"

"In that middle can." He eyed her carefully. "How did you like the bed?"

"Oh, I just rolled down into that valley in the middle and couldn't get out."

He drawled: "I seem to recall some kind of a kid story about a guy coming in and finding somebody in his bed remember it?"

"The Three Little Bears?"

"Yeh—that's it. And what was the gal's name?"

Her delicate lip curved. "Goldilocks."

He looked at her hair. "Well, Goldilocks. I see you've gone for a new color."

"The more to fool you with, my dear." She was cracking eggs, expertly dropping them in a dish, carefully stacking the shells. She greased the skillet with butter, put it under a slow fire. "When will our other guest be here?"

"Tommy? Oh, any time now."

She put coffee and water in the percolator, then she dropped the egg shells in. He said: "What's the idea?"

"Makes it settle. You seem interested in cooking."

"I'm more interested in the cook. I'm trying to see why the kid goes for you."

"You think he does?"

"Goldilocks, what does a guy have to do in your league to prove he's nuts about you?"

The coffee was on the fire, the eggs were waiting. She began to cut oranges. "Do you have a squeezer?"

"I usually do that with my hands."

Dan held a glass pitcher between his legs, squeezed the oranges with his powerful fingers until the juice had all run out, tossed the rinds at the sink. She asked: "Wouldn't he have done the same for any girl?"

"Let's make it any pretty girl. But I'd have more respect for the girl if she hadn't let him do it."

Her face and her voice were pained. "But I tried."

"All I know is that he almost mortgaged his entire life to bail you out of a mess."

"And you think I wasn't worth it."

"What else could I think?"

She faced him. "You're his friend. It's swell the way you've be-haved this morning. It's what I sort of expected you to do. I'd like you to believe that I haven't done—and won't do—anything to hurt him. Can you believe that?"

He looked down into her earnest face, "Frankly—no."

Her cheeks were as red as the fire in the stove. Dan said: "Sorry, Goldilocks, but you asked for it."

Her chin did not fall. Her eyes stared steadily into his, without a wavering thought, until a flush cooked up in Dan's wide, honest face. Then a light smile curved about her delicate mouth. "Would you mind setting the table?"

When Tommy Donati arrived they all sat down to breakfast. It was a pleasant and a hearty meal. They had orange juice, ham and eggs, fried potatoes, French toast, and coffee. All of them, including Ruth, did full justice to it.

"This reminds me of those bathing beauties the employment agency used to send around here." Terry grinned at Dan.

"Shut up—and pass that platter."

"Dan," Terry said to Ruth, "was going to put it on big when he took this place. No more greasy spoon restaurants, no more meals at phony clubs,—just a big hearty home-cooked meal every night. Well, this is the first one he's ever enjoyed—thanks to me."

"Thanks to you nothing—thanks to Goldilocks."

"Don't thank me," Ruth said, "this is the first chance I've had for a good meal in a week—so I made the most of it."

Breakfast over, Dan sat back and looked at his empty plate, passed his hand lightly over his belt, shook his head. "Maybe I got a break after all—that I didn't get a cook—three meals a day like this and I'd look like an alderman." He smacked his hands together with a re-sounding whack, looked about the table significantly, "Well, let's get down to business."

Ruth's eyes were upon her hands.

Terry said calmly: "Suppose you tell them, Ruth, how you hap-pened to go to work for Ramon—everything that occurred until the time you got on the train."

Ruth told her story simply, with obvious sincerity. She finished with exact details of her visit to the office on Sunday morning. Dan spoke for the first time: "Why didn't he send this letter by registered mail?"

"It was my impression that he didn't want to take any chance on the person to whom it was sent being identified. I think this will explain." She handed him the note Ramon had written to her.

Dan read it aloud.

When he had finished, he leveled his strong eyes at those of Ruth Allison. "Where's the other envelope?"

Ruth, frowning, looked at Terry Moore, who said: "Ruth thought she'd like to deliver that personally—and then let you quiz his wife."

Dan shook his head. "Guys who get themselves killed can't expect to keep their families out of it. We'll give her whatever breaks we can. Where's the letter?"

Ruth brought the letter from her bag, surrendered it with reluctant relief.

CHAPTER XX

Dan looked at the envelope, weighed it momentarily in his big hand. "Such a little thing—and yet it may mean life or death. . . ." His eyes went to those of Ruth Allison. She was sitting on the front edge of her chair, her lips slightly apart.

Dan shrugged, calmly ripped the envelope, dumped its contents in his lap. There was a one-sheet note, folded and eight one-thousand-dollar bills. He unfolded the note slowly, read aloud:

My Dear Rose:
I am sending this money to you by the only person I feel I can trust. Please take it. I earned it in a manner you may not approve, but it is mine. I suppose you will be surprised to hear from me after all this time, but I have been in a spot I couldn't get out of. Now I see a chance and am taking it. If all goes well, I will come back for you. If anything should happen to me, perhaps it may be better if you just take this money and try to forgive me, rather than make an effort to avenge me. The one decent thing I have done for you is to keep you out of this final sorry mess I have made of my life. Nobody knows that you exist except this girl, my secretary, who will deliver this. She knows nothing so do not discuss with her what happened at the Golden Pheasant. That might lead to trouble for both of you. But if anything should happen to me, you will

know it will be because of what I saw there that night.

But I do hope to see you soon.

Ray.

There was hushed quiet in the room.

Dan said: "I guess he wasn't the worst guy around." He smiled at Ruth Allison. "And I guess you're not the worst gal, Goldilocks."

She asked softly: "Does this clear it up?"

Dan answered: "Yes—and no. It fits in with everything we've got up to now—but it isn't evidence."

Terry was disappointed. "But doesn't it clear Ruth?"

"I'm satisfied that she's okay—and, after this, anybody would have a tough time convicting her—even if anybody wanted to. I'm satisfied that Johnny and Morgie knocked off the night watchman, although I don't know the reason yet; that Ramon, or Ray, saw it and they used it as a club over him; that he had to go along with them—although that isn't quite clear yet; and that he was going to use me as a means to break jail. All that is obvious enough.

"But," now Dan started to walk around, "this still isn't evidence that Johnny and Morgie committed either murder. It's the written word of a dead man who admits that he swore to a lie before—because it was he who gave Johnny and Morgie an alibi for the murder he now says they committed. So, we're in the same old spot they run up against in the detective movies—we know who did it but we can't prove it—and we can't prove it because the only guy who saw it is dead."

Terry protested. "But there ought to be some way—when you know who did it—"

Dan shook his head. "If everybody was in jail who we know should be there, there'd be a new government project for more jails. I'm afraid John is going to be hard to hook—unless we get a confession—and all we'll get out of him will be the bird. We used to have a way of handling. things like this—but that's out." He turned to his partner. "I guess the next step, Tommy, is to pick up this wife and see what she knows. Ray might have told her what happened—but even that would be secondhand evidence from a dead perjurer." He looked at the money in his hand, then at Ruth. "Do you think this was really his?"

"It could be, I know that he won consistently on his outside bets—and that didn't belong to Johnny."

Dan handed the money to Tommy. "Give it to the missus. It's probably the only insurance she'll get. We're not a collection agency for Johnny, anyhow."

Tommy, putting on his coat and hat, said: "It looks to me, Dan, like Johnny wasn't after money. He was after this envelope. It looks like Terry's idea might have been right—that Ramon told Johnny this evidence was on its way—that Johnny lost his head and killed Ramon and then tore after Miss Allison. It fits better that way. Johnny wouldn't keep his head in this noose for this kind of money."

Dan was listening carefully, as if he had respect for the occasional opinions of his partner who listened much and talked little. "Sounds all right," he admitted. "Well, you pick up the old lady and let us know what she says."

"Will you be here?"

"For awhile." Dan smiled. "I'll go over it with our new partners. Something might pop. They're pretty bright."

"So long," Tommy said.

When Tommy had gone, Dan looked at Ruth Allison. "In the meanwhile, the safest place for you will be jail."

Her eyes dropped and her shoulders slumped, but she said nothing. Terry protested, "No, Dan—"

Dan said: "If I could toss you in there with her, I'd do that, too. Johnny's a bad guy. He wouldn't mind pyramiding two more murders to save himself. He already had Ruth framed for Ramon's kickoff. You scared hell out of him, Terry, when he thought you were going through with that strip exposing the inside story—he was ready to knock you off then—"

Dan's voice trailed off and his eyes narrowed.

He walked about, making a tube out of one big hand, blowing through it against the other hand, as if this helped him think. He seemed to forget that the others were in the room as he walked out to the terrace, paraded up and down, as if to some slow music in his mind.

Ruth looked at Terry with sad eyes. "I don't want to go to jail, Terry."

"Maybe you won't have to— Dan seems to have some kind of a notion."

Dan stood in the terrace doors. "How much guts have you kids got left?"

"Enough," Terry replied. "For what?"

"In case we might want to play detective again. You know that gag where they get the guilty party in a room and play a trick on him and force him to confess?"

"Yes?"

"Well, it isn't that. Johnny goes to the movies, too. But he does have certain peculiar weaknesses, and it might be dangerous if anything went wrong—" He turned to Ruth Allison. "How are you on steaks?"

Her eyes were tearfully bright. "I'm afraid I'm awfully good on steaks, Dan—"

"That settles it!" Dan went to the telephone and called the building superintendent. "Hello, Mac? Dan Colby. Listen, Mac—have you got a maid's room empty in the basement? Yes, will you? I'm going to try another of those damned cooks."

The curtain rose on the last act of the Gambling Murder while the public was walking out of the theater, grumbling that this was another drama without a last act.

Ruth Allison had not been caught and nobody seemed to care. The Johnny Duke bombshell had proved a dud—and Johnny was still seen about the café belt, apparently entranced by glitter nostalgia. The story had been chased off every front page in town by newer, fresher crimes and the case was fast sliding into the muckish limbo of the unsolved.

Then, without preliminary announcement, the Little Hercules strip returned to the front page of the *Leader*. It was the beginning of a new adventure titled The Man in the Black Hat. The locale was a Broadway club called the Golden Pheasant, whose owner wore a black hat and looked like Johnny Duke; there was a big fellow with a hatchet face called Porgie; and a gambler named Ray Torse, who looked like Raymond Torrance.

The opening strip showed Ray Torse winning sensationally from the slot machines and the owner, identified as Black Hat, looking on suspiciously while he told his henchman, Porgie, that something was wrong—that the machines should not be paying out that way.

The strip caused curious comment about town and a marked increase in circulation; but the new series was generally regarded as merely another, if bolder, effort on the part of Terry Moore and Empire Features, to cash in on the fading publicity of the murder case.

The second strip showed the Golden Pheasant in darkness, with two men using flashlights, obviously tampering with the slot machines—while Black Hat and Porgie crept upon them.

There was a sharp leap in circulation for the third day's issue which revealed the conspirators as Ray Torse and the night watchman. It showed Black Hat, in insane rage, attacking the watchman with his fists—and Porgie killing him with a knife.

That night Dan Colby and Tommy Donati walked into the Café Ferdinand and went immediately to the table where Johnny Duke and Morgie Stern were having dinner. The meal-time chatter dimmed to quiet whispers. The only active noise in the place was the music from the piano. It might have been a scene in an old silent picture, scored with nickelodeon music.

It seemed nothing more than a chance meeting of friends. The gamblers were alert, Tommy was quietly unperturbed and Dan Colby was jovial. As he left he rubbed his big hand in a seemingly affectionate gesture across the bald front of Johnny Duke's head.

For a moment explosion threatened.

But nothing happened.

After that the situation fell into an absorbing routine pattern.

Each evening, at about eight-thirty, the *Leader* hit the streets with its new installment of The Man in the Black Hat.

Each evening Johnny Duke and Morgie Stern ate dinner in some part of the café belt, as if retreat would be a sign of weakness.

Each evening the word got around just where they were and the restaurant was crowded when Dan Colby and Tommy Donati arrived for their friendly visit.

Broadway was watching a new and curious type of man hunt, a psychological third degree obviously aimed at the unstable dynamo of Johnny Duke's nervous system. In its own lush accouterments, Broadway was seeing a streamlined melodrama of the old West, where a fascinated group watched the meeting of enemies in a bar, wondering when the shooting would start.

But after awhile Broadway discerned a further element in the plot, knew there would be no fireworks until Johnny Duke met up with Terry Moore, feared that when this did happen, it would not be in a public place.

For it was Terry Moore who was the real enemy of Johnny Duke, who was, in the parlance of the street, murdering Johnny Duke, tying him up with invisible cords, strangling him with printer's ink, setting up the climax of this new third degree.

Each day Terry Moore told his story in cartoons as effectively as from a witness stand. Through his eyes the town saw what happened at the Golden Pheasant; the switch of operations to Hollywood at the Cinema Circle; the birth of "Ramon Toros," the entrance of Ruth Allison, of Terry Moore and of Dan Colby; the argument at the Circle; the rebellion of Ramon; the visit of Ruth Allison to the office on the morning of the crime; the delivery of the envelope to her by Ramon.

The town accepted all this as fact; convicted Johnny Duke and Morgie Stern of the murder of the night watchman; and was now waiting for the continuance of the story, the murder of Ramon, the framing and flight of the girl, the pursuit by Johnny Duke—

The town was wondering who would write the final chapter— Terry Moore or Johnny Duke?

Wondering whether something might not also happen to Terry Moore—something as cute, as unsolvable, and horrible as had happened to the night watchman and Ramon Toros.

But it would not be easy. Terry Moore had removed himself from circulation. Nor could Kenny Tompkins enlighten his café intimates. All they knew at the paper was that, each day, the new Hercules strip came down from the office of J. G. Carson himself. Not even Carmichael knew how it got there or where Terry was.

Broadway finally had a show with a new plot, an absorbing drama with a fresh twist, a play with a last act.

CHAPTER XXI

Terry Moore was sitting in the one big chair in Dan Colby's apartment, working by the light of the reading lamp. He was putting the finishing touches to the strip for the next day—the strip which showed Johnny Duke and Morgie standing outside a window upon which was painted, in black letters, the words: Raymond Torrance, Inc.

Dan Colby was lying on the studio couch, his face to the wall, away from the light.

Ruth Allison's voice came from the kitchen: "How long will you be, Terry?"

"I'm about finished."

Ruth called: "Dan—get up."

The big detective rolled over, hands behind his head. "I haven't had any freedom around this house since we got a hostess."

At the table, Dan heaped his plate with a thick steak, mashed potatoes, and fresh lima beans. There was a salad of asparagus tips well covered with creamy yellow sauce. He ladled gravy over the potatoes, looked reprovingly upon the food. "Well, here goes the waist line again."

Ruth smiled. "I notice we never have to feed you."

"Like all women, you play upon my weakness."

Terry grumbled: "What're you squawking about? At least you get a chance to walk it off."

Ruth protested. "How about me? I'm growing out of this dress."

Terry said: "I wish you would grow out of it."

"One of these days I'm going out and buy a new one."

"Uh-uh—" Dan answered, "and wind up in jail."

"We might as well be in jail," Terry said.

Dan grinned. "I thought you two were happy here." When they did not answer, he asked: "What dessert tonight?"

"Lemon chiffon pie."

Dan groaned. "Four more pounds."

"Just the same, you'll be sorry when I'm gone."

"Maybe I will—but my waist line won't."

Ruth looked at him with the smile of the true culinary artist who knows that her work is appreciated. "How long do you think it will take, Dan?"

"How many more strips do you figure, Terry?"

"About six."

"Then it will be six days—"

She frowned. "I was hoping to get out by Tuesday—"

"Why?"

"That's my birthday."

"You'll miss it by one day—unless friend John makes a move before then."

Terry said: "I might cut the series short—"

Dan shook his head. "Now don't get rambunctious—either of you. As long as you follow script, everything will be all right. Well, where's that pie?"

The pie was two inches thick. Dan looked at it, said: "Well, if I must—" When he had finished he went to the radio, lifted the button. Tommy answered almost immediately: "Coming over now?"

"If I can make it— I've just had another of those World's Fair meals." He pushed the button down, choking Tommy's laugh.

When he was ready to leave, Dan fitted the envelope containing the strip beneath his topcoat, hesitated at the door. "If you're getting bored I'll bring home a checker game. Be good now, children—papa will be back around eleven."

When he had gone, Ruth and Terry cleared up the dishes and went to the tiny kitchen. She fitted him with an apron and they went to work.

Ruth was still wearing the old cotton dress, but her face was fresh and full again, the thinness and worry was gone, she was rested and radiant with health. She said: "I'm sorry if you're bored with me, Terry."

"You know I'm not. If we must be in jail, there could be worse ones."

"Except that you're tired looking at me."

"I didn't say you—I said I was tired looking at that dress. It's like—well, like weeds on an orchid."

She was shining the percolator, looking at its polished surface, a polish that had not been there when she had first come to the house: "Nice recovery, Terry—too bad you don't mean it."

"Sure, I mean it. So your birthday is Tuesday? Wouldn't it be great if we could go out and really celebrate with a dinner and a show and a club?"

"Yes—but you heard what Dan said."

"I'm going to be a mighty proud guy when I can first show you the town."

When she didn't answer, Terry continued: "You'll be a bigger curiosity than Judy Garland."

She laughed. "I'll be bigger, anyhow."

When they had put the last dish away, they went into the living-room. Terry said: "How about a little practice for your debut? We can't look bad when we make our bow." He got music on the radio. It was a rhumba.

She stood, swaying her hips, snapping her fingers, rhythm in her body and her blood, challenging life in her eyes.

They looked steadily, provocatively into each other's eyes, as the dance demanded. He said: "You were dancing the rhumba when I first saw you—remember?"

Her eyes clouded. "I remember. Terry—do you think this will really end all right?"

"Sure."

"But it's frightening. You don't know how I fear that man—"

"Dan won't let anything go wrong."

The music changed to a slow movement again. She dropped her head to his chest. His arm tightened protectively about her. She said, to his lapel: "In some ways I'll be sorry when this is over."

"Uh-huh."

"But I would like to get out for my birthday. I have always been a kind of a nut about birthdays."

"So have I. Well—"

They danced.

About eleven o'clock that night, Terry was on the terrace, smoking, looking at the river lights. He heard the rumble of the elevator and quickly returned to the house. Ruth was sitting in the big arm chair. They waited, alertly, until the door opened and Dan came in.

He grinned. "All you need is the family cat to look like an old married couple."

Ruth said: "We've talked over everything by now, I suppose. How was everything in the big city?"

Dan put his coat and hat away. "You might get out for your birthday yet. I think our fox is getting pepper-feet. He wasn't very sociable tonight. And he asked about you, Terry. Wanted to know why you never came out any more. He was very insulting, as if you were afraid. I would pop him if I were you—the first time I saw him."

"I'm not looking forward to it; but look, Dan, suppose he doesn't fall for it?"

"Well, then we'll just have to grab him and do what we can with what we have; but that will mean a long go with a good chance of his getting loose—and that's not to be desired—no, sir, not to be desired. Right now, I think John thinks and dreams nothing else but how to sink all of us without a trace. He was never so dangerous in the ring as when he was coming off the floor."

Terry protested. "What're you trying to do—scare us?"

"No—just sort of get you ready—kind of gas-mask practice." Dan acknowledged Terry's warning glance toward Ruth. He put his big hand on her shoulders. "Nothing to get scared of, Goldilocks. You'll have plenty of good men in your corner."

"I'm not frightened, Dan."

"Sure not—you've got the guts of a burglar."

Later, Terry and Dan said good night to Ruth Allison, circled the terrace, then crossed the roof and went to Terry's apartment. Dan entered first, turned the switch, and walked through the place with his hand in his right coat pocket. The blinds were down.

Terry said: "Dan, I wish this melodrama was over."

"Getting jittery?"

"Yes."

"Spoken like a man—but once the curtain rises, you'll give a great performance."

"Glad you think so, but this is getting tough on Ruth."

"I know—but that kid's got good stuff in her." Dan meticulously folded his trousers to protect the creases. Stripped, he was all muscle—and no pie.

"Took you long enough to find it out."

"Touché."

"Listen, Dan, I've got a hunch we shouldn't allow her to stay alone up there at night any longer."

"She's as safe as Gibraltar."

"That's not so safe anymore either."

Dan chuckled. "You talk like a guy the night before a big fight. It's a good sign."

"And you talk like a fight manager. While we're wearing Johnny down, what do you suppose is happening to my nerves—and Ruth's?"

Dan said: "Did you hear anything then? I'll lay you even dough Morgie's outside that fire escape right now."

"Well, you go look."

Dan chuckled as he went to the fire escape window, looked out. "Take it easy, kid—and if the worst comes to the worst—be thankful Johnny only uses his fists and Morgie just carries a knife."

"But he throws that knife, doesn't he?"

"I don't think he's so good at it. When he really wants to make sure, he has to get up close. Now get to hell to sleep, will you?"

"I haven't slept before daylight since this began."

"Well, you've got lots of time all day to catch up. In fact, you're living the life of Riley."

"And you still have a very peculiar sense of humor."

Dan turned out the light. His voice in the dark had a different note, a deadly serious note. "Terry—what do you suppose would happen to a guy in my racket who didn't?"

"Didn't what?"

"Didn't have a sense of humor?"

CHAPTER XXII

At four-thirty on Tuesday afternoon Terry Moore finished the last strip in the adventures of The Man in the Black Hat. He signed it, took one last long look, put it in an envelope and shook his head. He went to the kitchen door.

"Ruth—I'm going to drift down to my place for a little while—I need some new material."

A frown creased her face. Her face was thin again and there were lines under her eyes as if she hadn't been sleeping. "Careful, Terry."

"I will."

"I wouldn't want anything to happen to you—on my birthday."

He grinned. "Neither would I." She had been doing things to her hair, like a girl who was getting ready for a party. His fingers went impulsively to the edges of the black curls. "Your hair looks nice."

"Thank you. It hasn't had much attention lately—so I thought I'd do it up a little. Do you like it as well as the—other?"

"Better."

"You always say the right thing, Terry."

He smiled. "That's on the level—but one of these times—just once—I would like to see you in that red mop again." He looked at his watch. "What time do we eat?"

"Usual time—about six."

"I'll be back before that."

He opened the door a trifle, looked out, growled. "I'm beginning to feel like a public enemy."

It was after five when Terry returned. He was carrying his work-bag. "I've got an idea for some sketches—thought I'd work on them in my spare time."

She talked from the kitchen. "What kind of sketches?"

"Oh, some stuff for magazines. "I've had a few offers—but this is the first time I've ever had an idea." He moved out of her vision, opened the bag. "I'll fix the table, huh?"

"Thanks."

After a few minutes he called: "Ruth."

On her plate he had placed a white orchid. She uttered a soft cry, picked it up, held it for a moment against the swift color in her cheeks, just below the blue-blackness of her hair. "It was sweet of you, but you shouldn't—" Then, as if realizing what he had done— "You really shouldn't have done it. Suppose somebody had seen you."

His grin was boyish. "Nobody did. Go look in your mirror."

She went into the bedroom. He waited until he heard a soft cry of pleasure.

The elevator was coming. She came to the door, lips apart, eyes frightened. "It's early for Dan—"

"Go back."

Terry waited.

Dan and Tommy entered, each with an armload of roses. Terry called: "Ruth—"

She saw them, slowly shook her head—then tears came and she went back into the bedroom, closed the door.

Dan said: "What happened?"

Tommy Donati, who was married, smiled. "She's happy, you big lug—she's been on edge—now she's happy—so she wants to have herself a cry."

"That's a funny way to be happy."

"Women like to be happy that way."

Tommy started for the kitchen. "When they don't snap out of it right away—you can't tell how long. Terry—rustle up some vases—"

"He means vawses," Dan corrected.

They arranged the flowers. Tommy looked with somewhat practiced eye over the stove. "Seems like everything's ready to be served. Come on, you guys,—get busy."

"Doing what?" Dan complained.

"It's her birthday, isn't it?"

Dan said: "I still don't see what she's crying about."

"You'll learn."

"Not me. I know when I'm well off."

They all moved toward the kitchen. Dan got there first; but there was room for nobody else and he did nothing more than look at the food and grin. Tommy said: "Come on out of there—you weren't built for a kitchen mechanic. You rustle up the chairs—I'll dish it up and Terry, you take it in."

Dan agreed. "Sure—he's a well-trained husband. Jeeps—I never thought I'd wind up running a matrimonial agency."

The food was ready. They were waiting. Dan, inhaling odors, said impatiently: "This cry must be over the Derby route. Hey, Ruth— come and get it."

"I'll be there." There was no cry in her voice.

"She's all right," Tommy said. "Now there's one more thing we ought to do—sing Happy Birthday when she comes out."

"Sure," Dan agreed heartily, "let's go for the works. You be the m.c., Tommy."

The door was opening.

Tommy started to sing. The others joined:

> "Happy Birthday to you
> Happy Birthday to you
> Happy—"

The song tailed off.

Dan Colby swore a lusty oath.

Ruth Allison was in the doorway, an unexpected vision of white and gold. She was wearing a white lace dress that left her arms and shoulders bare. The white orchid, with its thin flute of wine, was at her shoulder.

She was wearing the red transformation.

Her face was blooming with milky health, her eyes shining with feminine ecstasy.

It was a tableau of male worship before startling feminine beauty. In this situation, when even a slavey would have been glorious, Ruth Allison evoked and accepted the tribute to a shining streamlined Venus.

She moved from the doorway, walked like a queen among them, preening herself in all that delirious moment which comes once to every woman, when she is a goddess before men.

Then she forsook the role and became a happy, excited girl. She ran to big Dan Colby, kissed him, paused shyly before Tommy Donati, kissed him, then went to Terry Moore, gave him her lips, her eyes, her arms, her heart.

All of them had hands on her chair as she sat. She bowed graciously. "I'll never forget you big lugs for this—" Then the tears came again.

"Hold it," Dan Colby cried.

Ruth shook her head quickly, smiled through misty eyes.

Dan Colby said: "All this fancy-doodle is too much for my nerves. Goldilocks—let me say my piece first—you're terrific." Then, as if embarrassed at this outburst, "Well, there's no reason we can't eat now, is there?"

A little later Dan said, apparently to the steak, "Imagine—an angel who can cook steak like this." He turned to Terry Moore. "Did I ever say you were dumb?"

"Yes."

"Okay—embarrass me."

Ruth blessed them with her eyes. "I'll be sorry to leave all this."

Dan looked up. "You don't think you're going to get away, do you?"

"When's your birthday, Dan?"

"July 13th."

Terry reminded: "It's awful hot up here in July."

"Hot or cold, Dan—it's a date."

"It's a date. We'll give a party—and invite the Commissioner." Dan chuckled at the thought of the Commissioner, then rambled on. "I never had a birthday party. They're all right. Tommy—we should have brought champagne."

"It's not too late—we'll bring it back after."

"Okay—and how about bringing Louise? Got anybody to stay with the kid?"

"She might make it."

Dan said to Ruth: "You'd like Louise—your kind of doll." He took another long look at her. "You wrap up swell, kid." His eyes narrowed. "Where did you dig up the outfit?"

When Ruth didn't answer, Dan's manner changed. "Did you go out today?"

"Yes, Dan—"

Terry said. "No—I did."

"Are you crazy? Didn't I tell you—"

"Easy, Dan," Tommy's voice was calming.

Dan said to Terry "Where did you go? I mean—every move you made."

"I went out the back way by the service entrance and through the garage. It was about four-thirty and there were a lot of people coming and going. I walked down Second Avenue to the bank—"

"What bank?"

"On the first floor of the *Leader* Building—"

"That was smart—"

"I didn't meet anybody. I went to my safety deposit box—"

"For what?"

"Something private—has nothing to do with this. Then I came back up 42nd Street to the flower shop on the corner and a dress shop next door, came back here and in by the back door again. I'm sure nobody saw me."

"They know you in that flower shop, don't they? And in the garage?"

"What if they do? I live around here. I'm not exactly a fugitive."

Dan said: "You shouldn't have done it."

"Maybe not—but it's done now. Even if somebody sees me—they'd look for me in my place—and what good will that do?"

Tommy said: "It's all right, Dan."

Dan went out on the terrace, was gone for five minutes. When he came back he bolted the door. His humor had returned. He grinned at Terry Moore, shook his head as at a contrary child. "I guess it's all right—only stay off that terrace and take no chances tonight—even if it is a birthday and there's a moon. We'll be back as soon as we do our boy scout's duty. We're too close to the finish now to have anything jam the works. Promise?"

Ruth said: "He promises."

When they were alone, Ruth said to Terry: "It was a beautiful thought, Terry—and I'll never forget it—but you really shouldn't have done it—just for a dress and a flower."

"But it wasn't just for a dress and a flower."

She went to the table, smoothed the roses, took the one that was in fullest bloom, walked toward him, a golden-haired girl in a white dress, carrying a red rose.

He said: "You look like an altar boy carrying a red candle."

He was sitting in the big chair. She stood before him, slipping the stem of the rose through his lapel, said softly: "A candle is a prayer. This is my prayer of thanks, Terry—for everything."

He caught her hand. She looked down at him for a moment, gently took her hand away, walked to the radio, got music. He came to her. She said: "I still don't understand why, Terry."

"For the same reason I wanted you to wear a white dress tonight. My grandmother believed that a person who came to her door might be an angel—and she never turned one away. That night, on the train, my grandmother seemed to be telling me that. That's why I wanted to see you in a white dress tonight—your face and golden hair above a white robe."

"Terry—you frighten me."

"That's why I went to the bank today—to get something that belonged to my grandmother."

He took her left hand.

She pulled away. "Please, Terry—it wouldn't be fair." She shook her head. "That belongs to Luella."

"I've thought all that out. My grandmother didn't send Luella—she sent you."

She was looking at the ring as he slipped it on her finger. She was whispering, "I shouldn't—I know I shouldn't—but I love you so—" Her head came up and her eyes were closed and her lips were tremulous and soft.

They stood there, together, as soft music filled the room.

Then they were thrown apart by the lightning of a snarl: "Lovebirds!"

Johnny Duke was in the room. Morgie was closing the terrace door.

It had happened, Terry thought, just as Dan had planned—except that Dan wasn't in the bedroom, Tommy wasn't on the terrace, and there were no other men on the roof or beyond the door.

CHAPTER XXIII

Morgie locked the terrace door. Johnny snapped: "Watch the other door—and the telephone. You two sit down—on that bed—give you a break. And don't move."

Terry and Ruth sat on the studio couch, watched as Johnny looked into the bedroom, locked the door, put the key in his pocket. He inspected the small kitchen, tested the closed window, then cautiously looked out in the foyer. Then he gave them his attention. "Gorgeous as ever, aren't you, sweetheart? Sort of surprised to find you in a spot like this—anybody that was as persnickity as you."

Morgie's hatchet face was strained. "Come on, boss. Last time—remember—"

Johnny's moldy eyes glared at Terry. "We changed the routine tonight, Hercules. We got tired having everybody in town watching us eat. We're having dinner in a private dining room at the Pelican right now—with people who will swear we were there all the time. We were seen coming in the front way—and we'll be seen going out the front way. You see, Hercules, it's like I told you before—I always have an alibi."

Morgie's heavy whisper interrupted: "Geeze—Johnny—hurry up— suppose Dan comes in—"

"He won't come in. He and Tommy will be in their car chasing from place to place looking for us—the wrong places—because they'll be getting bum steers." He turned savagely to Morgie. "And even if he does come—so what? If both of them come—so what? I'd like to see them come. Now shut up—will you?"

Morgie dropped his eyes.

161

Terry and Ruth were exchanging a still glance. Her lips slowly framed a rounded word—without a sound—a word like—radio—but Johnny's black eyes returned to them in time to catch the suggestion of the whisper. "What was that?"

She shook her head slowly, eyes upon him. He snapped, "Well, whatever it was, it makes no difference. Hercules, get one of those strips you draw on—you know—the kind you draw the pictures about Black Hat—" With acrid humor he pointed to his hat.

Terry got to his feet. Ruth arose also. Johnny grinned at her. "Not you, sweetheart. You just sit down on that bed again. You look good there." Her eyes caught his meaning; she swallowed and sat down again—near the radio, within reach of it.

The gurgle was in Johnny's voice again, the sex sugar in his eyes. "There, that's it, sweetheart, we'll come to you later. Long time no see. Okay, Hercules—get moving."

"My material is in the bedroom."

"Hmm. Bedroom, eh? Nice little time you've been having up here—kidding Johnny Duke. Well—go get it."

"You've got the key."

Johnny grunted, opened the door, stood on guard. Terry fumbled and stalled, made deliberately suspicious moves. He wanted to distract Johnny and give Ruth a chance to turn on the two-way radio and warn Dan, Tommy, or Headquarters. This was their only chance; but when he returned with the case, he saw that Ruth had not been able to get to the radio. Morgie's eyes were dead upon her, Morgie was taking no chances. He was anxious to get this over.

But Johnny Duke was in no hurry. His smirk was back. He stood beside Terry Moore, looking down at the cardboard strip. "I suppose you're wondering what we came here for—eh, Hercules?"

"You won't get away with it—I know that."

"Get away with what? Why, Hercules—what do you have in your mind? What do you think of that, sweetheart?" He turned toward Ruth, and the sardonic smirk became a snarl. "Get away from there."

Ruth was at the radio. She dropped a button and turned her back to it, as if attempting to hide the movement. Johnny roughly jerked her away, lifted the button. "Sit over in that chair and don't make any more moves—or I'll muss up that pretty kisser."

"I was only trying to get some music, Johnny." Her smile was friendly, femininely provocative.

Johnny sneered. "You'll get music—plenty music—when your time comes. So you thought you might keep me from hearing that elevator, eh, sweetheart? Still trying to outsmart Johnny Duke—"

Terry's stomach was sinking. Ruth had tried to establish connection with Dan and Tommy—Johnny had caught her at it. If she hadn't been so fumbling, so obviously slow! That was not like her. She was unnerved. And now she was making it worse, talking back to Johnny Duke in a loud, provocative voice that was also unlike her.

"Johnny Duke—you're mad if you think you can get away with this. Dan Colby and Tommy Donati are not out looking for you. They will be back here any minute—and they'll take care of you and Morgie."

Terry was shaking his head, warning her to be quiet. Their only chance now was to go along, not to antagonize him.

Johnny was saying: "Hear that, Morgie? She's giving us a break." He moved menacingly toward her. "That will be enough out of you. Keep an eye on her, Morgie. I've got business with my pal, Hercules."

Ruth sat back. She did not seem depressed. Her eyes were bright, sparkling with hope, as they looked at Terry and then gave the slightest inclination toward the radio.

Then Terry knew what she had done.

The button was up.

She had lifted the button as Johnny had seen her; to allay suspicion she had openly switched it off, hoping that he would turn it on again. It was lightning thinking, daring gambling. Johnny had himself established the connection. She had shouted provocative defiance to warn Dan, Tommy, or Headquarters not to answer, and thereby tip Johnny off that he was being overheard.

Ruth had set a new stage for confession. If Dan and Tommy were not in their car, Headquarters should have had the signal. If they understood Ruth's warning they would not only listen to what was said but would send help. If they did not get the warning, if an answering voice came into the room, anything might happen. Terry waited, actually breathless, for the radio voice that might be the signal for his death and Ruth's. The voice did not come.

Terry assumed that the connection had been made; that somebody was listening; that help was on its way. This wasn't the way Dan
had planned it but it might work out just as well. Ruth had done her
job. It was now up to Terry Moore to get Johnny Duke to talk, to stall
until help arrived.

Dan had said that when the time came Terry would give a great
performance. This was the time. It was either a good performance or
the end of living.

Johnny was facing him now. "I've been enjoying your series in
the *Leader*, Hercules. I read you were going to publish the last one
tomorrow. I thought you might need a little help with that one—that's
why—we dropped in this way—"

Morgie's-husky whisper was anguished. "You're wastin' time, boss."

But Johnny was in a cute mood, as Dan had predicted he would be.
His laugh was jovial. "The trouble with you, Morgie, is you've always
been just a mechanic at this business. Now I'm an artist—and an artist likes to do things up brown—isn't that right, Hercules?"

"You mean an artist at murder, Johnny?"

The word "murder" electrified the room.

First there was the stillness of absolute quiet; then the swift in-
take of Ruth's breath; Morgie's protesting groan—and the sharp crack-
ling laughter of Johnny's insanity, like the ominous sound of lightning
outside the window of a high building.

"Hercules, the trouble with you is, you talk out of turn."

"An artist likes to have his work appreciated, doesn't he, Johnny?
He likes to have people know about it."

"Keep talkin', Hercules. Keep stallin'. Maybe somebody will come
and bail you out—is that it?"

Dan and Tommy left the Stork Club hurriedly and entered their
car which had been parked just outside the door in the space reserved
for cabs. Their faces were set earnestly as Dan darted through the
traffic. "Where next?" Tommy asked.

"The Tavern."

Tommy said: "Look. The office is trying to get us." The signal light
was on. Tommy made the connection and was about to answer; but a
familiar voice came into the car.

"I guess there's not much hope of us getting bailed out, Johnny. You've got us in the same spot you had Bootsie and Ramon."

Both detectives were stunned.

Again came Terry Moore's voice: "As one artist to another, Johnny, I was just interested in how you did it—that's all."

Morgie's voice: "He's trickin' you."

Johnny's voice: "No, Morgie—this guy interests me. He always has. He's got a peculiar kind of guts and maybe he's giving me ideas."

Morgie's voice: "He's a cutie, Johnny—you know that. Let's get it over and get outa here. I'm hearin' funny noises."

Dan switched off the radio, stepped on the floor board, released the siren and the car screamed through traffic, through red lights.

Dan said: "You think they're getting it at Headquarters?"

"They must be."

"We can't listen or the noise would tip them off."

Dan cut under the Third Avenue elevated structure at 45th Street, just missing a truck.

Johnny was playing cat and mouse. His eyes were playing with Terry Moore's. "Another trouble with you, Morgie, is you've got no sportsmanship. Any guy who thinks he can outcute Johnny Duke ought to have a chance. I thought, Hercules, you knew all about everything—the way you drew those pictures."

"Not everything, Johnny. I never could understand just how Raymond happened in on that job at the Pheasant—"

"Uh-huh. And what else?"

"And why you were fool enough to kill Ramon—instead of just beating him up?"

"Uh-huh. And what else?"

"Why you're fool enough to think you can come in here and get away with this?"

Morgie groaned. "For Chrissakes, Johnny—"

"No, Morgie. He's asked some honest questions and I think he's entitled to an honest answer."

"But we ain't got no time—"

Johnny looked at his watch. "Hercules—how long does it take you to draw one of them strips?"

"About an hour."

"That means stallin' time. Well, I'll give you a proposition. If you keep workin' fast and do a good job, I might wise you up a bit—not that it will do you any good!"

"I'm just curious, Johnny—as one artist to another."

"Well, we might make a deal. Morgie—listen for that elevator. Hercules, you start drawing. I want you to draw a strip. When you finish it—mark it the end of the story. As one artist to another I'm going to give you the chance to leave something behind you that will be sensational."

Ruth's eyes were upon Terry."

Johnny continued: "Draw a strip in which Little Hercules and the girl are together; they are overcome with remorse; they have decided to end it all—"

Terry again was looking into the eyes of murder. Johnny continued: "But before they go, they want to make a confession; they want the world to know that it was they who killed Ramon and got away with his money; and they tried to pin it on Johnny Duke and Morgie Stern. Then Terry Moore and Ruth Allison will sign the confession in their handwriting. Then the last picture on the strip will show their bodies in the bottom of that court outside—a double suicide, a love leap—and Dan Colby can explain how they got there."

Terry started to get to his feet. "You're mad—"

Johnny pushed him back. "There will be no knife wounds this time—just two broken bodies—one of them very beautiful—and a swell picture for the front page of the *Leader* tomorrow—the best picture since Ruth Snyder—"

"I won't."

Ruth said: "Draw it, Terry. You must."

Johnny gurgled: "Yes, Terry, draw—and hustle it up. I'm getting hungry. Aren't you getting hungry, Morgie?"

Morgie was moving nervously. "Boss—you're actin' nuts again—"

Johnny swung back, laughing. "So I'm nuts again, am I? Everybody in here thinks I'm nuts."

"You told me to tip you off, boss—"

"Sure, I'm nuts. J. Duke is nuts. Just like when he caught that tinhorn cheating with those machines—that's one thing you didn't know,

Hercules—the guy was a wizard with machines—worked in the factory that made 'em. Nobody told you that, did they, Hercules—not even his wife that you gave that money to—too bad she isn't here, too—"

He swerved to Morgie. "So I'm nuts—just as I was that night when I used him for an alibi, then took him to the Coast for a shill and my machine man. You wanted to kill him, Morgie—remember—right off, just like you don't want to waste time now. But you're just a mechanic, Morgie. I'm an artist. And all artists are supposed to be nuts, isn't that right, Hercules?"

The room was a madman's stage and Johnny Duke was giving a performance.

"And I was nuts when I found out he was going to give me the cross with Dan; sure, J. Duke was nuts when he gave Ramon the extra jab with the paper knife that belonged to Sweetheart, and then put Dan on her trail. And that would have worked out, too, if Hercules here hadn't got stuck on the girl and put his long nose in it. Well, we're taking care of that now—but we're doing it with class—that touch of class that my pal Dan always talks about."

He leered at Ruth Allison, advanced upon her until his face was close to hers, but she did not quail. "Sweetheart, it's too bad you muffed the chance I gave you because you're pretty good—good enough to put Dan Colby on your staff—and that's something they've been shooting at for years around here. And Tommy Donati, the model married man. When I heard all of these guys had bought flowers this evening—I got nuts again. I took a little gander at your birthday party, sweetheart, and then I knew this would be a cinch. I intended just a quiet, neat little job."

He turned to Terry, laughing gently. "But Hercules here says I'm an artist. Kiddin' Johnny Duke again. Stallin' for time. But he gives me ideas—lots of them. Now, I've really got a honey. As one artist to another, Hercules, see what you think of it."

He backed against the door to the corridor, faced them: "So now what do we do? We don't jump over the garden wall. The lover's leap is out. We change things around and lump them all together. Oh, is this a masterpiece! First you draw the final strip, Hercules, end of the story—only now it's a double suicide by gun. Then when you've both signed it, I go to work. First, I do what I've always wanted to do all my life, Hercules—I beat a guy to death with my fists—you—and then, Sweetheart, I kiss you good-by—a nice, long kiss, Sweetheart—" The sex sugar was in his eyes.

Terry Moore was on his feet, tossing the board aside. Ruth cried: "No, Terry—no—"

Terry Moore was fighting for his life.

He struck out as Johnny rushed, felt his right fist connect solidly, heard Johnny's mad bellow and then felt the sting and the thud of Johnny's heavy hands.

He went down.

He saw Ruth huddled back against the wall, knew that Morgie was circling to get back of him.

Johnny's foot was kicking at his head. Terry grabbed the foot, upset Johnny Duke. Then he was on his feet again, striking out. He hit—and was hit. He landed against the wall, dazed, struck out blindly again, circling away from Morgie, who wanted to save time.

He saw Ruth coming from the kitchen with a knife—saw Morgie throw his own knife at Ruth—saw that the knife had missed.

"The gun, Johnny—the gun—" Morgie was calling as he picked up a chair and rushed at the girl. As Johnny's hand went to his pocket, Terry leaped upon him and they went to the floor together.

He saw Morgie swing the chair, Ruth's arm go up and the knife fall to the floor. He saw Morgie hit Ruth flush in the nose with his fist, saw her go down, bleeding.

Terry was all animal himself now. He forgot Johnny Duke's gun, threw himself at Morgie Stern, felt his right arm suddenly stiff as a sword, lash out at Morgie's face—

Terry heard a shot—felt a piercing pain in his left arm—thought that this was a perfect shame, that Dan and Tommy would probably be just *a little bit too late.*

There were other shots, of which Terry heard little.

Then, if that were possible, he heard a quiet. And out of it finally came Dan's hearty voice, a brotherly sort of voice, saying: "Snap out of it Slugger—you won the war."

CHAPTER XXIV

The last strip of the Gambling Murder cartoons occupied the entire front page of the *Leader* the next morning. It was drawn under difficulties because the artist was propped in a hospital bed.

As Johnny Duke had predicted, it was the most sensational picture since Ruth Snyder's execution. It showed Johnny Duke himself and Big Morgie Stern, cold in death upon the floor. It showed Dan Colby and Tommy Donati with smoking pistols. It showed Ruth Allison with her arms about Little Hercules, who was also on the floor.

In the corner, as requested by Johnny Duke, there was the printed legend: "End of the Story."

Luella gazed long at the picture, a puzzled look upon her classic face.

ABOUT THE AUTHOR

Francis Wallace (1894-1977) was a sportswriter, author, screenwriter, and sports commentator. A graduate of the University of Notre Dame, Wallace may be best known for writing the story that made Knute Rockne's "Win One for the Gipper" speech famous. Wallace wrote numerous fiction stories and non-fiction articles for different magazines, as well as seventeen books (almost all related to sports) and several movies. His boxing novel *Kid Galahad* was made into a movie twice—in 1937 and 1962 (the latter featuring Elvis Presley).

COACHWHIP PUBLICATIONS
CoachwhipBooks.com

COACHWHIP PUBLICATIONS
CoachwhipBooks.com

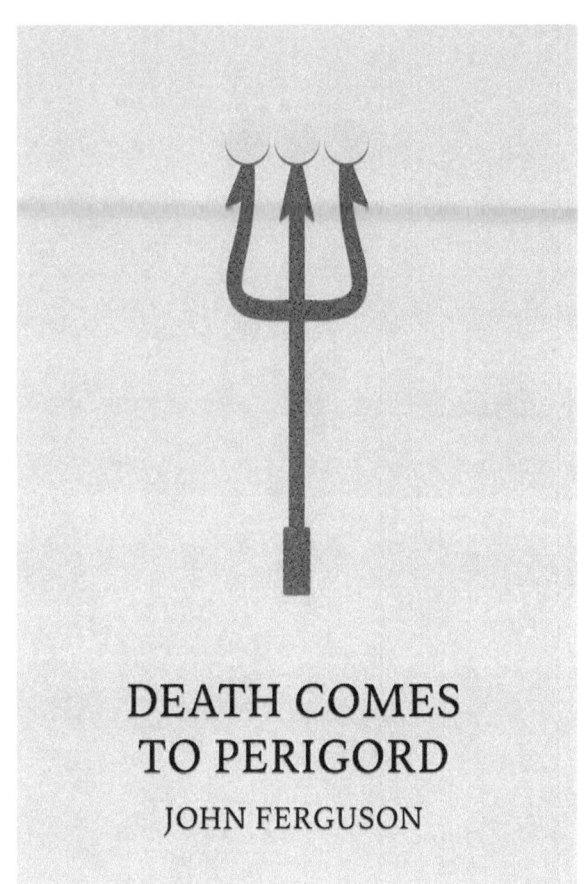

DEATH COMES
TO PERIGORD

JOHN FERGUSON

THE MYSTERIOUS WAYS
OF WANG FOO

SIDNEY C. PARTRIDGE

COACHWHIP PUBLICATIONS
CoachwhipBooks.com

THE INVISIBLE
BULLET

& Other Strange Cases of
Magnum, Scientific Consultant

MAX RITTENBERG

COACHWHIP PUBLICATIONS
COACHWHIPBOOKS.COM

PATTERN
IN BLACK
AND RED

FARADAY KEENE

COACHWHIP PUBLICATIONS
CoachwhipBooks.com

COACHWHIP PUBLICATIONS
CoachwhipBooks.com

THE SERGEANT HARTY MYSTERIES
JOEL Y. DANE

MURDER CUM LAUDE

1

THE CABANA MURDERS

COACHWHIP PUBLICATIONS
CoachwhipBooks.com

THE SERGEANT HARTY MYSTERIES

JOEL Y. DANE

GRASP AT STRAWS

2

THE CHRISTMAS TREE MURDERS

www.ingramcontent.com/pod-product-compliance
Lightning Source LLC
Chambersburg PA
CBHW020639250626
47154CB00008B/2739